For my son Omar, because of you I am not afraid.

Bittersweet

Evelyn C. Fortson

ISBN: 978-1-09837-216-3 (printed)

ISBN: 978-1-09837-217-0 (eBook)

Table of Contents

"By night on my bed I sought him whom my soul loveth: I sought him,
but I found him not." —Song of Solomon 3:1 (KJ)

Chapter 1

I had not thought about him for quite some time, but this morning I could not brush my teeth without my thoughts drifting back to the beginning when we had first met. I wonder if things would have been different, if I had met Wes before Naomi, would we have survived the rest? I like to believe we would have, but that may be me looking at life through rose-colored lenses again. I was not looking for anything, I just wanted to finally lose my virginity. I was almost 21 years old, and most of the girls I knew had lost their virginity years ago. So, I set out that night to do just that, I had not thought it through any further than lose virginity. I was not ready for the emotional storm that followed. I did not know then that most women could not separate their physical needs from their emotional ones. No one told me that lust had nothing to do with love. So that night what I thought would be a simple physical act, a lusty thing to be mounted and conquered, turned into something most tender and sweet. A thing to be nurtured and cherished. A thing that you brought home to your parents for them to examine and approve of.

I was completely lost in thought when I noticed the time on the microwave and quickly got up from the table, drinking the last dregs of my coffee, which helped to wash down the peanut butter covered bagel I was eating.

"Ruby, come on honey, let's go!" I shout, as I get her out of bed, and grab the clothes she will wear to school, and her backpack. Every morning I vow to leave the house in enough time to drop Ruby off at Valeria's house and drive to the train station without rushing, and every morning I am praying that I will not miss the train. After I put Ruby's clothes and backpack in the car, I remember that I left my cell phone on the charger so I go back into the house, grab my phone from the charger and run out the front door, locking it before I beep the car door open again. I look up at the early morning sky, which is blue black and dotted with twinkling stars, before getting into the car. Ten minutes later, Ruby jumps out of the car carrying her clothes and backpack. Valeria is used to our harried routine and is waiting at her front door, I wave at Valeria who is shaking her head, and speed off down the street.

The drive down the pass could either be a white-knuckle drive shrouded in thick fog or a relatively calm drive with bumper-to-bumper traffic. By the time I get to the pass the sun is coming up, so the sky is a hazy gray instead of black, the stars have disappeared, and only the faint outline of the moon remains. The mountains look like paper cutouts. The drive is bumper-to-bumper traffic and thankfully no fog. I spend my time in traffic in quiet retrospection. There is a poem, "Tis better to have loved and lost than never to have loved at all." As true as those words are, it is only after some passage of time that you can appreciate the sentiment. Life with Wes was filled with the sweetest pain, What should have been a time of self-discovery, getting my education and trying to figure out what I wanted to do with the rest of my life, became a time of fulfilling lustful desires, and subsequently, time spent trying to pick up the pieces of my life when my fairytale dreams of happily-ever-after came crashing down when someone else was having his baby. Even though those years with Wes did not yield the results I wanted, and sometimes they felt like wasted years, I am still glad I met him. I just wish it could have turned out differently.

I remember the first night we were together, twenty-seven years ago. It was at a friend's birthday party. I was hoping he would ask me to dance because I knew his reputation, and my plan that night was to sleep with somebody, anybody. After all it was the 80s; one-night stands were the norm. The party was breaking up and the DJ announced the last song, which was a slow song, I had all but given up on losing my virginity when Wes walked up to me and held out his hand, I put my hand in his and he walked me to the dance floor. Even though I had high heels on I had to look up to see his brown face. I remembered wanting to kiss his lips because they looked so soft, I placed my hands on his broad shoulders, as he placed his hands on my back pressing and grinding our bodies together. I held on to Wes and closed my eyes enjoying the world where only we existed. When the song ended, and the party lights were turned up Wes took my hand and walked toward the exit along with everyone else. He did not ask me if I wanted to go with him, and I did not ask where we were going. When we stepped outside, I saw Gina leaning against a car talking to some guy. I tugged on Wes's shirt and told him that I needed to let my girlfriend know that I was getting a ride home with him. Gina smiled as she looked over at where Wes was waiting for me. After I got into his car, Wes walked around got in the car, revved up the engine and pulled off in one fluid motion. I leaned back in the seat as the hot wind from the open window brushed against my face and ruffled my hair. Wes looked over at me when I began singing along with the song playing on the radio and smiled. I was smiling when he turned left on Imperial instead of right because that was not the way to my place. We ended up at his apartment, the living room was sparely furnished and what was there was either black or brown. The carpet was brown, the sofa was brown while the coffee table and stereo unit were black. I sat on the couch as he turned the stereo on low and sat next to me, kissing me softly until his soft kisses became urgent and hungry. Wes took me by the hands, pulling me up from the couch, while kissing me he walked me backward into the bedroom. Just as he laid me down on the bed, I saw a baby crib out of my peripheral vision. I knew I should have stopped, but it was too late for that, I feebly said no, but my legs kept opening wider and wider, then I stopped saying no and closed my eyes. In the dark, there were only the two of us and it felt like that was the only thing that mattered. He was so gentle while manipulating my body until my back arched, and my hips rocked in sync with his strokes. He began slowly, like the ocean waves lightly lapping at the sand, then the rain came softly at first; slowly becoming a raging storm, tearing up everything in its path; after the storm broke, he began to access the damage.

"Were you a virgin?"

I nodded yes. He just looked at me and smiled; that is when I noticed that he had dimples, and his smile caused me to smile.

Every time I thought we were done, he would slowly start up again, and my body complied. At one point there was a knock on the front door, but neither of us acknowledged that we heard it.

When the early morning light filtered through the curtains into the room and the baby's crib could no longer be ignored, I looked around the room. I could tell that a woman had decorated this room. The pillows on the floor matched the crumpled comforter at the end of the bed. There was a picture of a woman holding a baby, and a picture of Wes with the woman and baby. Just as I was wondering how I was going to get home Wes, asked if I wanted him to run a bath for me. Wes running a bath for me felt like a continuation of his lovemaking. As he ran the bathwater, I got out of bed and picked up my clothes. While I was soaking in the bath, I thought okay fine, I finally lost my virginity. I remembered thinking it was not the horror story that so many girls told about their first time.

Remembering Wes that morning almost made me miss my train. I caught the train just before it pulled out of the station. The Conductor must have been in a good mood because he did not close the beeping door in my face as he had done on other occasions, instead he stood looking at me from the next car, waiting for me to board the train. I made it to my court-room before the Bailiff opened the doors for the attorneys and the public to come in. The Judge had not made it in yet, so being his Judicial Assistant I opened the chamber's door and turned on the light making it look like he was in the building, as I was walking out of chambers my Courtroom Assistant came half running, half walking down the hallway.

"He's not in yet," I told her so she could slow down.

"Good. Sorry, I woke up late," said Frances.

I opened the private door to the courtroom for Frances to enter. Twenty minutes later the Judge buzzed me from the chambers to let me know he was in, I told him that we were ready to get started. A few seconds later the Judge enters the courtroom, the Bailiff announces that the court is in session and orders everyone to stand to be sworn. I swear in the audience and instruct them to be seated, and the morning calendars begin, only stopping for the mandatory court reporter's break and to allow the audience for the next calendar to enter the courtroom and be sworn. After lunch we continue with the trial in progress that looks like it will last more days than the counsel estimated. Between swearing in witnesses and marking exhibits, I continue to work on the minute orders from the morning calendar. At 4:30 p.m. court is recessed and the Bailiff watches counsel as they pack wherever they were taking with them, the Courtroom Assistant stores the exhibit books in the file cabinet and sets up the courtroom for the next day as I grab my purse, phone, travel pillow, my lunch bag and power walk down the back hallway connected to the Judge's chambers and begin the walk to the subway station. At Union Station I join the cattle stampede of people trying not to miss their connections from the subway to the train disembarking when I get to my depot. Three hours later, I am sitting in my family room sipping my cinnamon whiskey on the rocks. Why was the past pushing its way into my thoughts today? It began this morning and was only interrupted by work on the long train ride I was able to escape the memories because my train buddy and I talked all the way to my stop. On the drive home I called Nate and told him about my day, and he told me about his. I was almost at Valeria's house by the time we got off the phone. It was not until after dinner was prepared, consumed and Ruby was in her room on the phone with Danisha that thoughts of Wes came flooding back to me. If Nate, was at home instead of on the road maybe they could have been dismissed, like so many times before, but I knew I would have to deal with the memories that had pursued me all day. I sat in the family room, sipping my whiskey resigning myself to the inevitable reliving of the past.

Chapter 2

That first night together was the beginning of a lot of pain for me, but I did not know it then nor could I imagine what was to come from that impulsive decision, because all I felt that night was pleasure. After that night I did not hear from him and I did not expect to hear from him. It was clear from his bedroom that he and the mother of his child were together. So I was surprised that day when I entered my apartment to the sound of the phone ringing. I rushed to the phone before the answering machine could pick it up.

"Hello," I said.

"Hey, what's up?"

"Nothing much. What's up with you?"

"I can't call it. Can I come over?" asked Wes.

I hesitated before I asked if he remembered how to get here. He said he did, but he did not know the apartment number. After I hung up, I ran around the house picking up my clutter. I changed the sheets and took a quick shower.

The moment I opened the door the desire that was dormant re-emerged so strong that it was almost uncontrollable. We were rubbing and groping each other slowing the undressing of ourselves. After we were lay spent in my bed, Wes looked into my eyes and told me that he was living with the mother of his child, but that did not have anything to do with this. That we could see each other on the down low. I went along with what he was saying because at that time it did not affect me. I was not in a relationship with him, I did not have a child with him, and besides, he made me feel good, real, good.

In the beginning it was exciting and fun. Sneaking around made it that much more stimulating. We made love in the park, at the drive-in, on the beach, anywhere and everywhere, and I was like a moth attracted to the flame. Wes was my flame, and I drew closer to him basking in his warmth, hypnotized by the things he did to me and how he made me feel; and just like a moth I flew straight into the flame. Our meetings began to slack off after about a year. Instead of getting together several times a month, I was lucky to see Wes once a month. It got to a point when a couple of months would go by and I would have to call his mother's house so she could tell him to call me.

The transition from not being emotionally connected to becoming twisted up in something that I could not walk away from happened insidiously. Sometimes after we made love I would cry and he would take me in his arms and tell me, "We can stop anytime you want." Or he would say, "You knew the job was dangerous when you took it." And then he would make love to me and I would want him that much more. If only I had walked away when I realized that it was no longer fun, that this game I was playing was hurting me. The life I had before had disappeared. I made Wes my life without even knowing it. I stopped going out with friends, because I wanted to be available if he called or dropped by. My life revolved around whether or not he could get away, so I waited, and waited.

Wes called me at work one day and we agreed to meet up after work at my place. I was sitting at home waiting for Wes to come, the excitement that I felt earlier turned into disappointment then to anger. Finally, at 10:00 p.m. I got into my car and drove to Wes's place. That night was warm and unusually quiet, as I walked to his apartment unit, the only sound I could hear was the rapid beating of my heart. I kept telling myself it was not too late, I could turn around, but I could not stop. I guess I wanted Wes to make a choice. I wanted him to choose me. I knocked on the door, and Naomi answered the door.

"Is Wes home?"

"Yeah, he's here," answered Naomi standing in the door confusion clouding her face. "Wes!" she yelled while facing me, confusion slowly lifting. I could almost see the wheels turning in her head as the pieces fit together. The late nights out, the faint smell of perfume, maybe even a lipstick smudge or stray hairs on his clothes. Naomi turned to look at Wes when he walked in the room, she saw the same look of surprise on his face that I did. Wes immediately went to Naomi and wrapped her in his arms hugging her tightly as she asked him over, and over again who I was.

"I'm the woman's he's sleeping with," I answered for him. Naomi began to cry and struggled to get out of his arms, and I grabbed anything I could get my hands on. I picked up glasses, pictures, records and threw them on the floor while Wes tried to get Naomi to go into the bedroom. Cassius, Wes's little boy, walked into the room. I locked eyes with the cutest little boy. Cassius' cream-colored face with puffy jowls and big brown eyes, surrounded by a wild curly afro took the wind out of me, and I dropped the vase I was about to throw. It shattered into pieces on the floor, and so did my anger. I looked into Cassius's eyes and I was ashamed. I turned and looked at Wes. He was holding Naomi trying to explain me away, so I walked out the door, down the stairs into the warm summer night.

I drove home horrified that I could do such a thing. That night I sat in the living room of my apartment and tried to figure out how I got to this place. How could I be so desperate that I would eat the scraps left on the ground like a stray dog? What had I become? Who am I, I kept asking myself? I knew what I was doing was wrong and that is why I did not tell anyone about us. I did not tell my mother or my girlfriends. I never had a boyfriend growing up; I just, was not that interested. I remember thinking that this boy or that boy was cute, but I was a naïve kid who was not robbed of my childhood as other children were. I was not made to grow up fast because of something that was done to me. I lived the full length of my childhood believing in the Easter Bunny, the Tooth Fairy and Santa Claus. I believed the little white lies that parents told their kids, a little too long. I remembered believing in Santa Claus up until the seventh grade. My Mom and Dad never had the talk with me about the birds and bee. I never knew my value as a woman, or even that I could or should have placed a value on myself, because that was a modern concept that my mother had not known. My examples of male–female relationships were what I saw on television where boy meets girl, boy loses girl, boy reunites with girl and they live happily ever after. My parents were happily married but I never knew their love story. So, my crude relationship with Wes was romanticized in my mind, and instead of looking at our sexual attraction for what it was, I called it love. I convinced myself that I was in love, and so Wes must also be in love.

The next day I looked like hell. My eyes were almost closed shut from crying. I called off work sick because I was sick, I was sick of living a half a life. After that I did not hear from Wes for a long time. I thought it was over for us, and although it hurt, I was kind of glad it was over. After that night I closed in on myself, licking my wounds. The full measure of shame bore onto me. I was actively trying to destroy someone's family. Wes had a family, and it was not me.

One Saturday morning I noticed someone I had not seen before. He was alright looking; he was lighter than I liked and short for a man, but he had a nice size afro, and a nicely groomed beard. Later that afternoon just as the sun was beginning to set, there was a knock at my door.

"Who is it?" I asked through the door.

"My name is Jack; I'm your neighbor. I live upstairs."

I peered out the front window and saw it was the brother I noticed earlier. I asked what he wanted through the window.

"I'd like to invite you to dinner."

"Sorry, Jack, but I already ate."

"Well, maybe next time?"

I did not respond to that, instead I closed my blinds and pulled my curtains closed. I went to the kitchen and looked inside the refrigerator only to find apple juice, orange juice and a block of cheddar cheese. I poured myself a glass of apple juice in a wine glass, got Ritz crackers out of the cupboard and sliced several pieces of cheese for my dinner.

Sometimes I would see Jack at the mailbox, or by the car port, where we would speak to each other and keep it pushing. I started going to the gym just so I did not have to spend so much time alone in my apartment. Occasionally, my friend Darla and I would go to the movies or catch a play at the local playhouse theater, or Gina and I would go out to a club. My life without Wes had settled down to a boring, but comfortable routine. Saturday mornings involved cleaning my apartment, going to the gym, grocery shopping and then home. I was unloading my groceries from the car when Jack pulled into his parking spot and offered to help me bring my groceries in.

"I got it."

"I don't mind," said Jack, as he proceeded to pick up the rest of my bags and walked toward my apartment. I quickly closed the trunk and followed him to the front door of my unit. He stepped aside so I could unlock my door. He followed me in and placed the bags on the kitchen table.

"Nice place," he said as he surveyed my living room and kitchen. The living room consisted of a loveseat, a wicker trunk I used as a coffee table, and a bookcase that housed not only my books, but my family pictures and a small TV. In a corner of the living room by the front window was my prized possession, a large Ficus tree inside a woven basket. I have a couple of barstools at the kitchen counter, and a glass kitchen table and chrome chairs.

"Well, thanks for your help," I said as I ushered him out the door.

"Hey, I was thinking about putting some burgers on the grill for lunch. They don't take long to cook. Why don't you come up when you are through putting your groceries up? I'm in 2B."

"Okay, I'll be up when I get through."

Jack smiled and said okay as he walked out the door.

I put my groceries up and took a shower and changed into jeans and a T-shirt. I was not in the least attracted to Jack, but I was bored. I figured Wes and I were done, so I was going to at least try and move on with my life. Jack was grinning from ear to ear when he opened the door. It felt good to have someone so excited to spend time with you. It was then that I realized how lonely I really was. Jack and I stood on his small balcony. I sipped my soda as Jack flipped the burgers and toasted the buns. After the meat and buns were done, we went back into his apartment. I made myself two burgers, and sprinkled some chips on my plate, Jack had two burgers, a bigger mount of chips and opened another beer. We ate our burgers at the kitchen table. Jack was new to California; he was from Michigan. He had been in California almost a year, staying with his brother, his brother's wife and two kids until a few months ago. His apartment had a couch, a small wooden coffee table and a dresser against the wall with a TV on top. The kitchen had a wooden table with two chairs. Anyone could have lived there, as there were no personal items. No pictures on the wall, no photographs, no plants, just a place to watch TV and a place to eat. While I was not physically attracted to Jack, I really enjoyed talking with him. He was working at a plumbing company; he was not happy there, but at least he was employed. He had a three-year-old son in Michigan whom he missed and was hoping to be able to go visit next year. After a couple of hours, I thanked Jack for lunch and made my escape home.

Jack and I just sort of fell into a habit of having lunch or dinner together on the weekends. After a while we would go to the movies on the weekend and sometimes during the week, we would have dinner together.

I would knock on his door, or he would knock on my door, and we would spend the evening telling each other about our day.

We had a comfortable relationship except we had not had sex yet. It could have stayed that way as far as I was concerned, but one night in my apartment Jack and I had just finished sharing a pizza. I was washing the dishes when Jack came into the kitchen. I thought he was getting a soda or juice out of the refrigerator, but he stood there watching me wash dishes. I did not realize that he had not returned to the front room until he stood behind me, then I felt his hand slipping into my pants. I could hear his heavy breathing as he took his foot and pushed one of my legs to the side. I stood there frozen trying to decide if I should say yes or no. This man was not Wes, standing behind me was a man who openly dated me and shared his life with me. I knew this man was not sneaking into my bed but was coming openly to me if I would let him. So, I decided to let him have this moment, and I hoped that I would forget the man I desired to be with. I laid my head back and rested it on his shoulder, Jack turned me around and kissed me. Wes would have taken me on the kitchen counter, or up against the wall, but Jack walked me into the bedroom. As I laid there with Jack I wondered if men compared women as I was doing with Jack. My head nor my heart was in it. I even shut my eyes and tried to pretend it was Wes who was in my bed, but my body would not go along with the lie, and my nose could not be deceived. I did not have an orgasm and it was over before it started for me. I had always had an orgasm with Wes. I laid on my back thinking what have I done? I liked our friendship, but I could not do this again. Jack must have known because he got up and started to get dressed. I got up and begin pulling the sheets off the bed. It was not until he said I could have waited until he left to change the sheet that I realized how callous I was being. I did not mean to be unkind, but all I wanted to do was take a shower and get into my clean bed and forget what just happened. I did not say anything as Jack finished dressing and left.

After that night I would see Jack from time to time around the building. Gone were the days we talked about our day at work or made plans to catch a movie or a meal. I missed my friend Jack, but I could not imagine lying down with a man and feeling absolutely nothing. Jack made me aware that it was not just sex I had with Wes it was more than two bodies lying on each other. With Wes it was like two ribbons fluttering in the wind twisting onto each other, unwinding and winding back together; the ecstasy created by the touching of the ribbons caused them to flutter more and more rapidly until they broke free of each other and floated calmly away.

After that night with Jack, I knew that I should have gone to him and told him the truth, but instead I waited for him to come to me, but he never did. One night I was determined to speak with Jack to see if we could still be friends. I went up to his apartment and knocked on the door, but he was not there, or he would not answer. I knew we risked our friendship hoping to obtain something better, but all I wanted to do then was to salvage the friendship. A few nights later I saw him going upstairs to his apartment, so I ran up the stairs. This time when I knocked, he answered the door, but stood blocking the entrance to his apartment. A coldness had come between us. Jack told me he was busy and that he would catch up with me later. Later, never came for us, so on the nights I did not work late I came home and sat in my apartment missing two men that I wished I could have in my life. The loss of my friendship with Jack was much easier to get over, but that only made me focus my thoughts on Wes, back where I had started. Coming home to my empty apartment was becoming so depressing that I started going out drinking during the week and clubbing almost every weekend. I was becoming the person in the club who was trying too hard to have a good time. I was allowing any man who would dance with me or buy me a drink to get too familiar with me, some even thinking they could bed me down after one drink, so I went back to my routine of work and home, and an occasional girl's night out with friends from work. One Saturday afternoon I was sitting on my loveseat watching TV when a truck pulled into the driveway and stopped by the stairs. Jack and another man jumped out of the truck and ran up the stairs. Jack and the man begin loading his furniture and boxes into the truck bed. Jack did not have a truck so it must have been his brother or one of the guys he worked with. I opened the door when Jack was putting a box in the truck.

"Hey, Jack!" I said smiling at him.

"Hey."

"What's going on? Are you moving?" I asked before he walked up the stairs.

"Yeah," he answered never stopping to look me in the face, continuing up the stairs.

I waited for him to come back down. The man that was helping him move nodded a greeting at me as he placed another box in the truck. Jack and the man passed each other, and Jack hesitated slightly when he saw me still at the bottom of the stairs.

"You're not going to say goodbye to me?"

Jack stopped in front of me and finally looked at me. "I'll see you around."

"Okay, then if that's how you wanna be. See you around." I said turning to go back in inside.

"What do you mean, if that's how I wanna be?"

"You know what I mean. Even though that…night didn't work out, we can still be friends," I said facing him again.

Jack walked up to me and looked me up and down before he replied, "I'm not interested in being your friend, Eloise."

We stood and looked at each other. I wanted to get back what we had, and he wanted more than I could give. Jack's friend or brother came bouncing down the stairs with another box, breaking the standoff. Jack went back up the stairs and I went back inside my apartment. After a while, the truck pulled away and Jack's car followed. At least there would be no more uncomfortable meetings around the building.

Chapter 3

One night a noise jarred me out of my sleep, not because it was loud, but because it was so soft, I was not sure if I was dreaming or if it was really happening. I lay in my bed waiting to see if I would hear it again, when the beating of my heart slowed, I heard a soft persistent knocking at my front door. I got out of bed and slowly went to the door afraid to turn on the lights. I peeked inside the peephole and there he was. Wes was standing there with one hand on my door, his head hanging down. While I was still looking through the peephole trying to decide what to do, he looked directly at me. Did he see my eyeball through the peephole? If he did, he never stopped knocking on my door. I knew if I opened that door, I would have to go back to waiting and longing for a chance to be together. I would go back to living a secret life, only becoming fully alive when I was with him. I quietly took the chain off, slowly unlocked the deadbolt and opened the door. We stood there looking at each other, I stepped back, and he came in.

"You can't do that shit again." Was the first thing he said.

"I know."

He walked into the bedroom, I locked the door and followed him. He was sitting on the edge of the bed.

"Come here, baby," he whispered.

Wes did not make love to me that night, there was nothing loving about it, he was punishing me or his self for coming back. I should have stopped him, but I could never deny him, I did not have it in me. That night I was like a neglected garden that had finally been watered. The dryness of the months before were forgotten, and I splashed around in his waters, trying to slow him down, because I needed this night to last, I needed to wet every part of me. When it was over, Wes explained to me for the first time why he would not leave his son.

"I grew up without a Dad, so I told myself that I would never do that to a kid of mine."

"You can still see your son without living with his mother," I stated.

"I don't want to see my son; I want to raise my son."

"I get that, but are you trying to tell me that you're only with her because of your son? Do you love her?"

"Look, man, you're not going to like the answer, but yeah, I love her. We've been together since high school."

"Then, why are you here with me?"

"Because we're good together," he said as he brushed his fingers across my belly. "I like you. You're different from the other women I've been with."

"Other women!"

"Yea," said Wes grabbing me so I could not get out of bed. "Look you're the one who wanted to talk, so let's talk. Do you want me to be honest or do you want me to lie to you? You're not the first woman I stepped out on Naomi with. When I got with you, I didn't mean for it to go any further than that night, and I tried not to come back after you pulled that shit at my place, but here I am. So, what do you want to do?"

"I want you Wes, just you and me."

"I can't do that. I am not going to let another man raise my son. If you had come first, I could see us together, but it didn't happen that way. Look, Eloise I can go, and try not to bother you again, or…" Wes let the sentence float in the air waiting for me to fill in the blank.

"Or…we can continue to see each other like this." I stated.

"That's right," said Wes just before kissing me, talking that statement as an acquiescent.

He was right. I had agreed to his terms without putting up a fight.

I tried not to think about Wes and Naomi together; I tried not to think about the things he did to her. I told myself I was special and that he only did those things to me. When Wes was not with me, I told myself that he was only with Naomi because they had a child together and I told myself that one day he would leave her because just like in the movies the boy always got the girl and they lived happily ever after. The lies I told myself was how I justified what I was doing. In my heart, I knew Wes was with Naomi because he wanted to be, and he was with me because he could. Just as the lies I told myself began to wane Wes would come to me, filling me up with hope that one day we would live our lives together.

I will never forget that Saturday morning that exposed the lie I was living. I woke up early like any other Saturday. The sunlight was filtering through my bedroom curtains. I lay in bed watching millions of tiny little white dots floating in the air. As my eyelashes fluttered, so did the floating specs. The world was quiet, and a peacefulness enveloped me. When I opened my eyes the surreal world disappeared, and I dragged myself out of bed and put the coffee on. Every Saturday I woke up hopeful that Wes would be able to spend a little time with me, so I got up early and cleaned my apartment in between running back and forth to the apartment's laundry room either putting a load of clothes in the washer or the dryer. After I had ironed by clothes for the following week, I was restless, nothing good was on TV, so I decided to call Wes' mother's house hoping that he would be there.

"Hello," said Ms. Nola.

"Hello, Ms. Nola, it's Eloise is Wes there?"

"No, is he on his way?" she asked.

"I don't know."

"Well, did he tell you he was coming over today?" asked Ms. Nola slightly annoyed.

"I haven't spoken to him today...that's why I'm calling you," I explained.

"Eloise, ain't Wes with you?"

"No. Why would you think he was with me?"

"Oh, I just assumed since Naomi left you guys were together."

Before I could respond the line was dead. *What the hell,* I thought.

I sat there with the phone in my hand trying to make sense out of what I had just heard. If Naomi had left, why hadn't Wes told me? Why wasn't he here with me? A part of me knew then that something was wrong. The fear that began in the pit of my stomach travelled up to my heart as I grabbed my purse and keys. As I was driving to his apartment, questions occupied my mind making it difficult to concentrate on driving, did Naomi find out that we started up again? When did Naomi leave? Why did she leave and why hadn't Wes said anything to me? Did Wes blame me? The traffic was light, and soon I was turning onto the street Wes lived on. I parked the car and walked to his apartment. I was rehearsing what I was going to say to him to convince him that given time, Naomi would allow him to see his son or maybe he could get joint custody of his son. I was hopeful that after we talked Wes and I would be okay, so I knocked in rapid succession on his door.

The door was opened by a woman I had never seen before. She stood with one hand on the doorknob and one hand on her hips. She was beautiful. She was taller than me with skin that looked like caramel, long black hair, full bosom, narrow hips, and long legs that ended with stiletto clad feet.

"Yeah?" she said, more as a question than a statement.

"Is Wes home?" I asked, but before she could answer, Wes appeared at the door. He told whoever that was that he got it. She released the doorknob and backed up. Wes stood in front of me and forced me to back up with his body and closed the front door. We stood there on the small landing looking at each other.

"What's going on? Your mother told me Naomi left...so, who is that?"

Wes hung his head before he answered my questions. I looked at his plush soft lips as he told me that Shapira was a girl from the hood who he went to school with.

"A few months ago, me and the fellows went to a strip club. Shapira was one of the strippers there. At first, I didn't recognize her, but later when she came over to the group, hustling the guys for drinks and other services, I remembered her. She gave me a lap dance, and one thing led to another. Me and the guys went back to the club a couple more times and that was it. A few weeks ago, my boy Melvin told me that he saw Shapira at the club and she told him that I needed to come see her. I told Melvin I was done with that trick, but the next time Melvin went to the club she got belligerent and told him that if I didn't get in touch with her, she would go visit my mother and let her know she was going to have another grandbaby." Said Wes, as his eyes danced around my face unable to look into my eyes.

I continued to look at Wes's lips. They continued to move but I did not hear a word after "another grandbaby." I felt myself sliding down. Wes wrapped his arms around me pulling me up, and I laid my head on his chest and cried. We stayed out on the landing for a while. I leaned on him crying bitter tears, too weak to push away, Shapira opened the door and started yelling, "Who the fuck is this bitch? Who is this, Wes?"

Wes turned slightly and told Shapira to go back into the house. He tightened his hold on me and with his free arm pushed her back inside and closed the door never letting go of me with the other arm.

"Come on," said Wes as he walked me down the stairs. We walked down the street to my car.

"Eloise, I'm sorry, I fucked up…hey, hey look man, you know I can't let her raise a child of mine alone. Naomi went back to Detroit when she found out about her. She'll get tired of a baby…and maybe... Baby, please don't let this change anything," Wes said looking me in my eyes this time waiting to see if I would fill in the blanks again.

"Maybe, what? You fucked a whore, got her pregnant and I'm supposed to understand? Oh, and I'm supposed to do what…raise the fucking baby you had with a fucking hoe? I'm done, I'm fucking done!" I yelled as I pulled away from him.

I got in my car, and as I was driving home, I cried, because I was angry. Yes, I was hurt, but anger would be what motivated me to do what I would later regret. I remembered thinking that this time I was the one walking away, and the anger I felt made it easier to do.

The next few weeks went by like before except there was no relief from the monotony of going to work, home and back again, except for the gym. The aerobic classes freed my mind from thinking about what a fool I had been. I even bought an exercise bike, so I could exercise at home.

I remembered going to work one day with a black pencil skirt and a pretty, floral blouse which had ruffled sleeves and tied at the neck. I thought I looked good, up until I bent over to pick up the pen I dropped and heard my skirt rip in the back. Thank goodness I kept my workout clothes in the bottom file cabinet. I went to the bathroom and put on a pair of sweatpants. I kept my blouse on so I would look professional during the afternoon trial, as long as I did not leave my desk area. Even when I stood to swear in the witness, no one could see the bottom half of me. I managed to remain seated for most of the afternoon.

That night when I got home, I took off my clothes and looked at myself naked in the bathroom mirror. My breast looked the same, I contorted my body around to look at my buttock, then it dawned on me why I was getting bigger. I draped a bath towel around me and checked the calendar hanging on the wall in the kitchen. I always put a smiley face on the date that I had sex with Wes, and there it was, I had not had a period since the last time we had sex five weeks ago. I sat down at the kitchen table knowing that I was not going to see this pregnancy to the end. I could not be pregnant at the same time as Shapira. If there had not been a Shapira, I probably would have kept my baby, but I did not want to be that girl, pregnant by a man with multiple baby mommas and worse yet pregnant at the same time as another baby momma. The anger I felt that day when I found out about Shapira had not lessened, and the possibility that I was pregnant now only made me irate, it should have been me not Shapira living happily ever after with the father of my child. I sat at the kitchen table, brooding over the loss of Wes, and a child that my pride would not let me have until it was time to go to bed. The next day I called my healthcare provider and made a doctor's appointment. After it was confirmed by the doctor that I was pregnant I called Planned Parenthood and scheduled a date for the abortion.

I had not seen Wes since that day at his apartment, but I needed someone to drive me to the clinic. I drove over to his apartment rehearsing what I was going to say to him in my head. Wes was my only option because I did not want anyone to know that I was going to have an abortion. The baby I carried was now a part of the dirty secret that was our relationship. When I got to Wes's apartment I did not care if Shapira answered the door or not. If she had answered the door, I would have told her that I too was pregnant. I wanted her to know that her pregnancy, her position was not special. I pounded on the door, wanting her to answer the door, or at least know that I was there.

"Who is it?" Wes asked.

"It's me, Eloise," I answered.

Wes quickly opened the door and stepped outside.

"What do you want, Eloise?"

"I'm pregnant. I scheduled an abortion for next Wednesday and I need you to take me to the appointment and drive me home," I said quickly in one breath. I remembered standing there waiting for a reaction, instead all he said was okay and asked what time.

The days that I had to wait before I could end my pregnancy were days full of uncertainty, should I end my pregnancy? I waited for Wes to call, I found myself waking up in the middle of the night in a panic struggling to breathe. The anger that had sustained me was slowly slipping away and despair took its place because Wes had not asked me to have his baby. The day that I aborted my baby, Wes picked me up in plenty of time for the appointment, we did not talk much on the way to the clinic. I sat in the front passenger side of the car with my forehead pressed against the window. I soon found myself remembering a certain day when I was a little girl. I was sitting on the curb in front of the house I grew up in, a place that was so much more than a house, it was home. My legs were stretched out in front of me so my tennis shoes would not get wet. Someone was washing their car up the street and the water was running down the curb in front of me. I could hear the muted sound of a lawn mower in the distance and smell the freshly cut grass. I remembered being so happy in that moment looking up at the sunlit sky, with whipped cream clouds, the warmth of the sun on my arms and face. I sat there that brilliantly beautiful summer day, a voice within me told me to remember this quiet moment, the voice told me to remember the sound of the lawn mower, the smell of the grass and the warmth of the sun. The voice told me that this moment would sustain me in my darkest hour when life got too heavy, and suddenly an incredible feeling that exceeded happiness flowed through my body. The voice that was within me was no longer within but was with me on the curb enjoying that sunny day with me. It was not until I was older, and I was introduced to the concept of God, that I knew it was God that had shared his joy with me that day. So, even on that drive to abort my baby the memory of that day brought me peace in my darkest hour. When we arrived at the clinic I checked in with the receptionist and waited with the rest of the people gathered in the waiting room. The room had a quiet hush charged with tension as death hovered. There were women there with the men who had impregnated them, or with their girlfriends who they could trust to keep their secrets. I sat waiting for Wes to take me out of there or for my name to be called, I kept telling myself it was not too late I could always just leave, but I did not leave, and Wes did not take me from the place that would kill what we had created, so when my name was called, I got up and walked through the door without looking back.

Once I was undressed and lay on the examination table with a paper gown on, legs in the stirrups, I was told to relax and to breathe. I felt a pulling in my abdomen and a slight cramping, then the doctor patted my leg and said he was finished. After the abortion Wes drove me home in silence. He pulled into my apartment driveway and parked the car in front of my door. He came around opened the car door and helped me out of the car. Once inside, my apartment he asked me if I needed anything, I told him no I was good. He kissed me on the forehead and left. I stood by the door and watched him walk away. Just before he got in the car, he looked at me and smiled, and I felt the sun on my face, the pungent scent of freshly mowed grass and I saw a pretty, little black girl sitting on the curb looking up at the sky, and for a moment I was happy. The sound of the car door being closed brought me back to my front door and I watched Wes back out of the driveway.

I made myself a cup of tea, put on my pajamas and got into bed with a book and my tea. I fell asleep reading my book and woke up startled by the sound of a baby crying and a room full of shadows. After a moment I realized that I was in my own bed, the man on the other side of the room was my coat hanging in the closet and there was no crying baby, I prayed that God would forgive me, even though I knew in my heart that I would have made the same choice.

I woke up the next morning relieved that it was over, and I told myself that I would never put myself in that position again. I did not return to work until the following week. I busied myself with work and going to the gym and occasionally going out to the club, a play or dinner. I was regaining the life I had before Wes. I was not angry with Wes or myself anymore. Although I was alone, I was not as lonely as I once was.

Sultry summer days with clear blue skies gave way to beautiful sunny days with billowy white clouds, the warmth of the sun felt good on my skin, but the shade held hints of colder days to come.

I loved everything about the fall season, the crisp cool sunny days, cool enough to justify wearing a sweater, but too warm for a coat. Withering leaves blown across the street by a phantom burst of wind, while some trees are cloaked with an array of colors from the palest greens, yellows, oranges and browns before their leaves, too, are blown away. I was enjoying nature as I ate my lunch in the plaza area just outside the courthouse. It was the Wednesday before Thanksgiving and tomorrow I would be leaving Los Angeles and driving to Nevada to spend Thanksgiving with my parents. It had been six months since I terminated my pregnancy, and six months since I saw Wes. I wondered if his second child was born yet. I was looking forward to seeing my parents again. After lunch I finished my minute orders from the morning's calendar and caught up on my backlog and left work with a sense of relief because I was all caught up and could start Monday with a clean slate.

After work I finished packing for the long weekend and decided to go to bed early, so I could get an early start in the morning. The next day I woke up just before sunrise, showered, dressed, fixed coffee and got on the road. I loved driving to Vegas early in the morning, my mind was able to slow down as the desert flew by in the side windows but remained a constant panoramic picture in my windshield. As the miles went by, my mind began to think of Wes, I wondered if his second child had been born, and I wondered if he was happy. When I got to Barstow, I exited the freeway and pulled into a gas station. I used the bathroom, splashed water on my face, paid for the gas and continued, on the second leg of the trip.

I pulled into my parent's planned community, tired and needing to use the bathroom again. My Mom opened the door before I rang the doorbell. She was still in her nightgown, robe and house shoes. I hugged her and gave her a big kiss before I dashed into the entryway bathroom. When I came out Mom was pouring herself a cup of coffee and asked if I wanted a cup. I poured myself a cup of coffee and we sat down at the kitchen table and talked about the drive up and the plans for the day. I got my suitcase out the car and went upstairs to my room. I sat on the edge of the bed when it struck me that my baby would have been a newborn, Mom and Dad would have been so happy to have a little one to spoil. I was suddenly so tired I thought about lying down on the bed to rest for a little bit, instead I went back downstairs. Mom was just taking the biscuits out of the oven, and bacon was sizzling in the skillet. Mom set the hot tray of biscuits on the counter and went to the refrigerator for the eggs.

"You want eggs?" asked Mom.

"Yes, please."

"Scrambled?"

"Yes, thanks, Mom," I said as I sat at the table and waited for the bacon and eggs to be ready.

"You look tired; why don't you take a nap after breakfast?" asked Mom looking at me while cracking eggs into a bowl.

"I might lay down after I get the dishes, decoration and the chafing dishes set up."

After Mom and I ate breakfast Dad came downstairs. I was putting our breakfast dishes in the dishwasher when Dad made his way down the stairs. My Dad is so cute you just want to pinch his cheeks and rub his round belly. I put the plate I had in my hands in the dishwasher and met Dad in the middle of the family room where I gave him a big hug and a kiss on the cheek. Dad wobbled over to the kitchen table, and my Mom got up and made him a plate. All those years of marriage and my Mom still took care of my Dad like she must have done when they were first married.

I watched my parents as I finished cleaning the kitchen before I got Mom's fine china out of her china cabinet. Although the dishes were clean, I rinsed them because they had been sitting in the china cabinet since last Thanksgiving. After setting the dinner table, I sprinkled fake autumn leaves on the table and lay sprigs of faux red berries around three orange candles on the dining table. In the family room I set up the banquet tables and put the harvest inspired tablecloths on the tables before putting the chafing dishes and serving utensils on them.

Mom and Dad both admired the table settings. Every year I brought the decorations for Thanksgiving, and every year the décor was different. Even though I am an only child, Mom and Dad always had people over for Thanksgiving. Mom was in the kitchen checking her turkey, and Dad was sitting on the couch in the family room watching a football game. I told Mom to go upstairs and get dressed while I made the dressing and cooked the rice. I asked Dad if he was going to change and he told me he was changed. I laughed because we had that conversation every year. My Dad was dressed like Farmer John. He had on overalls and a plaid short sleeved shirt. Mom came downstairs freshly showered and dressed in tan slacks and a red sweater. I loved to see Mom in red. It is her favorite color, and it looks good on her. Mom has a soft salt and pepper afro, and she had put on a dab of red lipstick which looked nice on her. I told her that the dressing was in the oven and the rice was done, so I went upstairs for a little bit. Once inside my room I lay down and immediately went to sleep.

I woke to the sound of laugher and the smell of food. I changed into brown corduroy pants, a burnt orange sweater that I loved, and brown boots before going downstairs. When I got downstairs there was a young man watching TV with Dad. Mom was standing in front of the oven stirring her giblet gravy. Dad introduced me to the young man he used to work with. Dan was having Thanksgiving with us because he had to go to work later that night, and his family was back east. My cousin Brenda, her husband and kids were expected any minute. I heated up the water for the chafing dishes and filled the chafing pans with hot water before putting the food in the dish that the water would keep warm.

Just as I finished putting food in the last dish, the doorbell rang. Brenda and her family had arrived. They live in Vegas, so they visit my parents often and always have Thanksgiving with us. Brenda's two kids ran to Dad yelling, "Hey Paw Paw!" as they both tried to sit on his non existent lap. Dad balanced a kid on each knee, and Mom came out of the kitchen looking for her hugs and kisses. Brenda and her husband said hello to Dan and shook his hand but hugged and kissed us. Sam sat next to Dad on the couch and asked who was playing on TV. Brenda asked if there was anything, she could do to help so, I asked her to help me put the turkey on the platter. My Father turned down the volume of the TV and we all held hands as he said grace. Brenda and I served everyone buffet style. The guys ate dinner in the family room and watched the game while women and kids ate in the dining room.

"Gurrrl, what's going on with you?" asked Brenda.

"Nothing much, what's up with you?" I asked.

"You know, just the same old same old. Between the kids, work and the house, you know, I'm tired," responded Brenda. For the next 15–20 minutes Brenda droned on and on about her life never requiring more than an occasional grunt, moan or "Gurrrl." I caught Mom's eye and smiled. I am grateful for Brenda and her family filling my parent's life with the love that only little kids can give. I knew my parents were getting older, but I did not worry because I knew Brenda was there. Dan left shortly after dinner because he had to go to work. Brenda and I finished washing the dishes, and Sam broke down the serving tables in the family room and put them in the garage, afterward Sam and the kids sat on the couch watching TV, while Brenda and I finished putting up the dishes. After a while, Mom and Dad went upstairs to bed before Brenda and I finished with the dishes. Brenda and I joined Sam and the kids in the family room, watching TV until the movie ended. It was almost midnight by the time I closed the door to Brenda and her family.

The next day, I got up early and had my first cup of coffee in peace and quiet, but before I finished my second cup Mom came down the stairs still in her gown.

"Hey, Baby," said Mom.

"Good morning."

Mom poured herself a cup of coffee.

"I'm fixing pancakes, bacon and eggs after I finish my coffee," announced Mom.

I smiled to myself because my mother's southern roots were show-ing. Whenever I spent time with my parents, I had to be careful not to use their colloquial language such as fix instead of make or tote instead of carry, and I'm finna instead of I'm going to. It was easy to slip into their speech pattern because it reminded me of my childhood, warm, loving, and comforting to my soul. I did not know that people born and raised in the north did not speak like my parents until the kids at school made fun of my accent and the words I used.

I watched Mom as she made breakfast, and my heart skipped a beat as I realized my Momma was getting old. Her face was wrinkle-free, but the skin under her chin sagged. I could tell that yesterday took a lot out of her. While my Dad slept in, my Mom never stopped going and doing.

My Mom had always made the holidays special. Easter, birthdays, 4th of July, etc., every holiday, our house was the gathering place. I remem-bered the Saturdays of my childhood, friends and family came over to the house. The adults hung out in the house playing cards, drinking and lis-tening to music, while the kids played outside and stayed out of grown folks' business. At some point in the day the kids would be called into the house for either sandwiches or hot dogs, chips and Kool-Aid. The adult voices sounded like my parent's, and they used the same words that the kids at school teased me about using. When I did catch a bit of their conversation, it was always about a place they called "back home." I got the impression that it was a place they missed but was glad that they had left. I was roused out of my reverie by my Dad coming downstairs. My Dad was getting chubbier and chubbier every year, but today I noticed that his eyes did not have the mischievous glint they usually had instead his eyes were cloudy and filled with moisture, which he constantly dabbed at with his handkerchief. After breakfast, Dad asked me to go for a walk with him. Dad is competitive about everything, even things that would not normally be a competition, so I knew that this walk was really a challenge to see who could walk the longest. Dad and I walked outside the border of their planned community and turned right until we reached a planned walking path located next to a manmade riverbed. I was getting tried, so I knew my Dad was tired. I kept asking him if he needed to rest, and he would look at me and ask me if I needed a break. Finally, I conceded, and told him I needed a break just so he would stop and rest. By the time we made it back home, a little bit of that boyish glint was back in his eyes, but the fact that he went upstairs to rest did not go unnoticed.

Mom and I decided to get the Christmas decorations out so we could decorate the house for Christmas before I went back home.

Saturday night after we came back from the casinos, I said my good-byes to my parents before they went to bed. I liked to leave early in the morning, but I did not want to wake them, besides Mom would cry, and Dad would dab at his eyes more than usual, so I started sneaking out before they got up.

Sunday morning just as I am getting ready to go downstairs, Mom came out of their bedroom and asked if I was getting ready to leave. I gave Mom a big hug and hung on to her a little longer than usual and kissed her on the cheek.

"Call me when you get home." She said.

"I will, Mom. Love you."

"Love you, too, Baby."

"Go back to bed, Mom, I'll lock up on my way out," I said as I started down the stairs. I make it to my car when the thought that my parent may never experience the milestones of my life such as my wedding, grandkids, coming to my home for the holidays struck me. All those thoughts are going through my mind when I looked up and saw my Dad in the upstairs landing window waving goodbye to me. I waved goodbye to my Dad who had transformed for a brief, moment into an old man before I drove off.

Christmas came and went, then New Year Day marked the end of the holiday season, and I was glad it was over. I packed up the few Christmas decorations I put out and spent the rest of the day watching television on the couch. Just as I was trying to decide what to do about dinner the phone rang.

"Baby come get me," yelled Wes. "That bitch killed my son. I'm gonna pop that bitch."

"What? Wes…what happened? Where are you?"

"I'm at my Mom's. Come get me."

Whatever else he said I did not hear because time slowed down and collapsed as I sat on my couch listening to Wes yelling for me to come.

"I'm on my way," I said and hung up. I sat on the couch trying to understand what I was feeling. Finally, I got up and got ready to go. I was debating with myself if I should take a quick shower because I was still in the sweats, I rolled out of bed in. I opted to brush my teeth but not to shower or change my clothes.

On the drive to Ms. Nola's house my emotions went from concern to anger. I had not heard from Wes for almost a year. His baby would have been two or three months old. When I got to the street Ms. Nola lived on, it was packed with cars and people. Wes and his boys were standing in the yard smoking and drinking. I could see Wes talking to one of his boys as I drove past. I found a parking place at the end of the next block and walked back up to the house. Wes was in the yard when he saw me walking up the street. He held up both arms in the air and came walking toward me with a big smile on his face. I could see in his eyes that he was on full. Just before he got to me, he stumbled and spilled a little of his drink from his solo cup. Wes bent down so he could look me in my face. He was grinning and telling his boys his baby was here.

"Hey, man, this is my baby. My baby is here now," Wes said as he wrapped me in a bear hug spilling the rest of his drink. His hug turned into a collapse and I almost fell backward from the weight of him. Melvin came over and hugged Wes while pulling him off me.

"You good, man? What's up, Eloise? You here to take my boy home with you?" asked Melvin.

"I hadn't planned on it," I stuttered.

"Come on, man, take him home. He's all fucked up right now. I'll tell Ms. Nola you got him."

Wes started pulling himself away from Melvin and hugged me while asking if he could come home, and Melvin was looking at me like dude take him home, so I said okay. We staggered down the street back to my car. In the car Wes told me that Shapira had the baby three months ago and she was already back getting high and leaving the baby with her mother while she ran the street when he was at work. During the night he was the one who took care of his son, as she complained about being bored and wanting to get back to work.

"Last night I came home, and she was drinking and watching TV. I peeped in on the baby, I didn't turn the lights on in the bedroom because I didn't want to wake him. After I ate dinner, the baby was still asleep, so I asked Shapira how long had he been asleep and she said it had been a minute, so I went back into the room, turned on the light and looked into the bassinet. He looked so peaceful; his mouth was slightly open, but I didn't hear him breathing and I didn't see his little chest moving. I touched him so I could wake him up; his little body was hard. I picked him up and called 911..." said Wes trying hard not to cry.

I brushed tears from my eyes, not knowing what to say. The rest of the drive home was in silence except for the muffled sound of Wes crying.

That night he went right to sleep and did not wake up until almost noon the next day. After he ate, Wes showered and put back on the same clothes he had on the day before, and I drove him back to Ms. Nola's house. Ms. Beulah, a friend of Ms. Nola's, was sitting on the couch next to her. They had been friends for over 40 years and were complete opposites. Ms. Beulah's hair was beginning to gray around the edges of her round chocolate face, while Ms. Nola's hair was dyed red, pressed straight, except for the hair flipped up just before it reached her ears. The red of her hair complimented her cream-colored skin and softened her chiseled face. Ms. Nola was visibly shaken, she looked up enquiring into Wes's face when he entered the living room.

"How you doing baby?" ask Ms. Nola.

"I'm good, Momma, and you…you good?"

"I'm okay, son," she responded.

"Hello," I said.

"Hi, baby," said Ms. Beulah. I did not hear a greeting from Ms. Nola. Wes and I sat in the two chairs flanking the couch. Wes and his Mom began to speculate about what happened. Ms. Nola was trying to hold it together but was losing the battle. Tears are running down her cheeks. Ms. Nola wiped her eyes and face with a tissue. Ms. Beulah got up and told her friend that she was making her a cup of tea, then asked if we wanted tea. We both declined, and Ms. Beulah left the room. Wes told his mother that he was going to be stay at my place for a few days. He gave his mother a kiss and my phone number so she could call if she needed anything. Wes gave his mother another kiss on the cheek before leaving. Ms. Nola looked in my direction and nodded her head.

Once we were outside Wes told me that he would see me later after he got some clothes from his place and handled some business. He got into his car, which was parked in his mother's driveway, and I got into my car and drove home. Wes got to my place after dark, when I tried to get him to eat something, he said he was not hungry. We stayed up long into the night talking about his deceased baby, Wesley Jr., and how he had not seen Cassius since Naomi left.

Wes told me that Shapira was at his apartment when he went to pack his clothes, drinking and smoking with her friends. He told me how he physically had to kick her out of the apartment, after her friends finally took her away he packed Shapira's clothes in trash bags and took them to her mother's house. Shapira was not at her mother's house when he got there with the clothes, but her Mom told him it was wrong to kick her out when she was grieving the loss of her baby. Wes told her Mom not to worry, she would not be grieving for long if he found out she killed his baby.

That night we lay in bed whispering to each other as if we were sharing secrets. Wes told me about the son that he would bury in a few days and the son that he had not seen for a year. I did not share my feelings with Wes that night because his pain was too fresh and what he needed from me that night was for me to listen, understand and reassure him that everything was going to be alright. The next morning was overcast and it drizzled all day. Wes lay around most of the day; he called the detective working his son's case but was told he was not available. Wes left a message for the detective to call him, then he called his Mom, and updated her on the situation regarding the detective, I could hear him telling her that he would be over tomorrow. After he hung up, I sat on the couch next to him, he laid his head in my lap. We watched TV in silence until he fell asleep.

As I sat there listening to him breathe the hope that I thought had died begun to sprout in a dry desolate corner of my heart. In the midst of so much pain hope was taking root in my heart, Wes was there with me, something that I thought would never happen, something that I did not think I wanted any more. I sat in the darkened living room saddened by the price we both had to pay to be there – the death of an innocent little baby. I knew it would be my last chance at a life with Wes. Wes was snoring when I eased myself out from under his head. I replaced my lap with a pillow and went to the kitchen to prepare dinner.

Little did I know that my time with Wes would be so short. Had I known I wonder if I would have gone to him when he had called. Wes son's body was released after the autopsy, which was two weeks after his death. The coroner determined that the baby died of sudden infant death syndrome. Wes and Ms. Nola arranged for the services although Wes would ask for my opinion and even agreed with some of my suggestions. I took three days off work prior to the funeral so I could help with anything that needed to be done. It was decided that the repast would be held at Ms. Nola's house, and because the house was not big enough to accommodate all the people expected to attend, tables and chairs would be set up in the backyard. Wes had the gardener cut the grass, trim the hedges and put some grass down to fill in dirt patches in her backyard. Tables and chairs were ordered, and flowers brought for the tables. Food was ordered to supplement the food that the church ladies had provided. Paper plates, napkins, plastic utensils and cups were provided by Ms. Nola's church. I vacuumed, changed sheets, cleaned the refrigerator, ran to the store to pick up any forgotten items and did anything else asked of me. I was sitting at the dining room table drinking Ms. Beulah's sweet tea and eating a turkey sandwich when Naomi and Cassius walked through the front door.

Ms. Nola let out a yelp of delight and stretched out her arms, which Cassius ran into. Naomi's smile faltered a little when she saw me sitting at the table. Ms. Beulah got up from the couch and gave Naomi a hug, after which Naomi walked over to Ms. Nola and gave her a hug and kissed her on the cheek. Ms. Nola was overjoyed with seeing her grandson and Naomi. Ms. Nola got up and walked into the kitchen to make sandwiches for her grandson and Naomi. Naomi, Cassius and Ms. Beulah followed Ms. Nola into the kitchen, while I remained seated at the dining room table and struggled to swallow the sandwich which was stuck in my dry mouth. I had been so caught up with the funeral arrangements that I had not thought about Naomi. I could hear Ms. Nola yelling for Wes to come into the house, she had something she wanted to show him. I walked into the kitchen just as Wes walked through the back door. Cassius knocked over his juice as he scrambled out of his seat. Wes grabbed him and threw him up in the air a couple of times, and then held him tight against his chest walking out the room passing me with his head down still holding Cassius. The rest of us remained frozen in the kitchen until Cassius came back into the kitchen and hugged his mother.

"Da Da crying," he said holding onto his mother his eyes brimming with unshed tears. Naomi picked him up and told him that daddy was just, glad to see him. Cassius leaned against his mom looking perturbed. Ms. Beulah mopped up the spilled juice, the room was quiet now; the only sound was the hum of the refrigerator until Wes came back in the room and grabbed Cassius from his mother's lap.

"Come on, man, I need help in the backyard," said Wes as he carried Cassius out the back door.

Ms. Beulah recovered first and asked Naomi about her trip. I realized that I was still holding my empty glass and plate in my hands, so I walked over to the sink and put them in it. Not knowing what to do next, I went back into the front room. I sat in one of the chairs in the living room. I could not go home because I rode there with Wes. Ms. Nola, Ms. Beulah and Naomi came into the living room, Ms. Nola and Naomi sat on the couch close to each other, and Ms. Beulah took a seat at the end of the couch. Naomi and I had yet to acknowledge each other. Ms. Nola broke the awkward silence by telling Naomi to get her luggage out the car.

"You and Cassius can sleep in Wes's old room," said Ms. Nola.

"Thanks, Mom," said Naomi.

Naomi got up and went out the front door. Ms. Nola was sitting there with a sly smile on her face, and Ms. Beulah was flustered not knowing what to do next. Naomi came back into the house rolling two big suitcases with her and went directly to Wes's old bedroom. Wes came back in with Cassius asleep in his arms.

"Put him in your room," instructed Ms. Nola.

Wes carried Cassius to his room where Naomi was and stayed longer in the bedroom than I thought was necessary. Not wanting to seem insecure I sat there looking crazy while Ms. Nola's sly smile blossomed across her face as she looked directly at me. Wes and Naomi eventually come out of the bedroom, and Naomi took her previous seat back on the couch, Wes sat on the arm of the chair I was sitting in, and the conversation centered around the funeral service and reception for the next day until it was time to leave.

"Okay, Mom, we'll see you tomorrow. The limousine will be here at 8:30 a.m. so we'll be here about 7:00 a.m.," said Wes as he walked over to where his mother was seated, bending down to kiss her forehead. Ms. Nola looked up, feigning surprise that he was not spending the night.

"Won't you change your mind and spend the night so you can spend some time with your son?" asked Ms. Nola in her sweet as pie voice.

Naomi shifted in her seat and smiled slightly before looking down at her hands in her lap. Wes looked at me and said he had not thought about that and wanted to know if I would be okay with spending the night. Ms. Nola promptly responded with where would I sleep?

"Babe, I'm good. Why don't you stay and spend time with your son?" I stated.

"I'll drive you home. I need to get my clothes and stuff," said Wes.

We got up to leave, Ms. Nola and Naomi both were smiling up at Wes.

Once we got in the car, Wes wanted to know if I really was okay with him spending the night, and I told him I was and that it would be good for Cassius to have him there. We drove home in comfortable silence. Wes listened to the radio while I tried to figure out what Ms. Nola and Naomi were up to.

When we got home, Wes was going back and forth between the bedroom and bathroom, packing what he needed for that night and the next day. I sat in the living room looking in the direction of the TV, but not really watching it. Finally, I got up and went into the bedroom.

"You got everything?" I asked.

"Yeah, I think so," replied Wes.

"Well, if you forget anything just call me and I'll bring it tomorrow." I said as I walked up to him and hugged him. Wes hugged me back and I began to suck on his neck trying to give him an old fashion hickey. I wanted to leave a mark on him so Naomi and Ms. Nola would know exactly what when on at my place. I began to kiss him and caress him, and it was the first time we were together since his son died.

After Wes left, I took a shower, put on my pajamas and lay in bed with a book trying to get some rest before the long day tomorrow. I found myself having to re-read whole paragraphs because my mind kept wandering back to Ms. Nola and Naomi. Was Naomi planning to come back now that Wes was freed of Shapira? Would Wes choose me or Naomi and Cassius, was the last thought I had as I finally drifted off to sleep.

The day of the funereal I arrived at Ms. Nola's house a little before 7:00 a.m. Naomi opened the door and let me in. Wes was asleep on the sofa and I woke him up and told him the time. While Wes was in the bathroom, I cut the flowers for the tables in the backyard. After the flowers were arranged in the vases and placed on the tables I went back in the house to find Naomi pouring coffee for Ms. Nola, who is seated at the kitchen table with Wes and Cassius. I felt like an outsider watching a family eating breakfast. Wes looked up at me and asked if I wanted something to eat. I declined and told him that the backyard was all set. The doorbell rang and I offered to get the door.

Ms. Beulah was at the door dressed in black with a cute little pill box hat on top of her head. I hugged Ms. Beulah and told her that everyone was in the kitchen, then I went to the bathroom. When I returned from the bathroom everyone was in the living room. Cassius was running back and forward between his Dad and Mom. From the living room window, I saw the limousine pulling up in front of the house. Naomi must have seen it too, because she announced to the room that the limousine had arrived. Ms. Nola got up to get her jacket from her room, Naomi went to pack a toy and a snack for Cassius; Wes picked up Cassius and held my hand. When Ms. Nola came back into the living room, she pointedly looked at Wes holding my hand and asked if there is enough room in the limousine for all of us, which of course there was.

"Yeah, Mom, there's enough room," Wes said, and it was my turn to look like butter would not melt in my mouth and smile coyly.

In the limousine Ms. Nola was flanked by Ms. Beulah and Naomi; Cassius and I flanked Wes when Cassius was not in his father's arms. The traffic was horrific, as we knew it would be. The conversation was subdued and mundane until Ms. Beulah asked Naomi how long she was staying. That got my attention and my head immediately turned to look at Naomi.

"Oh, Ms. Beulah, I'm not going back! Well, I am going back, but that's only to pack up my stuff and come back here. Mom wants me to stay with her until I can get a job and get myself together," said Naomi looking directly at me. Wes looked at his Mother, Naomi and then at me.

"That's nice. I know Cassius will love being around his Dad and Grandma," said Ms. Beulah smiling at her friend. "Nola, you didn't tell me your grandbaby was coming back for good. Ain't that something, him living in his daddy's childhood room! I know you're happy about that! Look, we're pulling up at the church now, but before we get out, I want to pray," declared Ms. Beulah.

"Of course, of course," said Ms. Nola.

Ms. Nola clasped her friend's hand, and everyone else held the hand of the person closest to them. I was holding onto Wes's hand as I slid over to hold Ms. Beulah's hand.

"Father God, we thank you for waking us up this morning, clothed and in our right minds. We ask you to strengthen Wes and Nola today as they lay their son and grandson to rest. Lord, we know that he is in your loving arms, of that we are sure. Father, we pray that you comfort the living that are left behind, Lord, you said you would comfort the broken hearted. Thank you for your strength, which is needed to get through this day and the days to follow. I pray that the service today will be done in decency and in order. In Jesus' name. Amen," concluded Ms. Beulah, as the rest of us echoed, "Amen."

Wes got out of the limousine first and helped the rest of us out. Wes took Cassius from Naomi's arms and put an arm around his mother's shoulders. People were still walking into the church and occasionally one and two people stopped to say hello to Ms. Nola and Wes. Shapira and her family were standing outside the church. Wes walked over to Shapira and her family and invited them to join our group. The Pastor came out of the church and asked if we were ready to start.

Shapira and her family joined us, and Wes indicated to the Pastor that the families were ready. The double doors of the church opened, and the Pastor led the procession, head bowed in prayer. The service was short, because there was not a lot to say about a life that had ended too soon. The Pastor preached a sermon about how it was God who numbered our days, and how no man knew the hour of the Lord's return, before pleading for the unsaved to accept Jesus Christ as their Lord and Savior. A few brave souls accepted Christ, taking some of the stint of death away because Wesley Jr's short life was not in vain, souls were saved at his service.

After the last song was song, and the last word preached, the casket was opened for the viewing of the body; the family remained seated in the front pew. After the viewing was over for the public Wes walked up to the casket, and Shapira joined him. Shapira did not look like she had a baby three months ago; there was no baby fat anywhere. Her attire was more appropriate for the strip club then for the funereal service of her child. She had on a shiny silver halter top, a pale gray mini-skirt and stilettos. Her makeup was stage ready and her weave was on point. Wes looked down at his son and was either talking to him or to God. The funeral director and staff were standing to the side of the casket preparing to close it, but Wes placed his hand on the casket lid saying one last thing to his son before he closed the lid. Shapira cried out and Wes put his arm around her. The funeral director and staff placed the blanket of flowers back on top of the casket and gave instructions to the pallbearers. The pallbearers were the same guys I saw with Wes at his mother's house the day his son died. Melvin and the rest of the guys put their white gloves on before they lifted the casket and carried it to the hearse.

When we got back into the limousine everyone was quiet, even Cassius was subdued. Wes leaned against me holding my hand. We got out of the limousine for the graveside service, already emotionally exhausted from the church service. At the end of the graveside service people were given white balloons to release. Wes handed me a balloon to release as he and Cassius released their balloons. Finally, we made it back to Ms. Nola's house. The church ladies had set out the food and some of the guests were already eating. Ms. Nola and Beulah remained in the living room while the rest of us went to the backyard. The repast lasted into the night until only a few hardcore friends and family members remained. The ladies were in the living room and the dining room while the men young and old were outside drinking and talking. I was in the kitchen with Ms. Nola's church ladies, packing up food, washing dishes and returning containers to their rightful owner. After everyone had gone home Wes walked his mother to her bedroom then went into his old bedroom where his son was asleep, when he came back into the living room, I stood up to leave. Wes told Naomi that he would see Cassius tomorrow and said goodnight before we walked out the door.

After the funeral Wes divided his time between work, spending time with me and Cassius. Naomi and Cassius were still living with Ms. Nola, and Wes still had his apartment, although he spent most of his time with me. Naomi was adamant that Cassius could not spend the night at my place and preferred that I did not come along with Wes and Cassius on their outings. I did not have a problem with that; I thought Wes and Cassius father-son outings were cute, but sometimes I felt jealous of Wes's love for Cassius. I knew that Wes would lay down his life for Cassius. I knew Wes could walk out of my life without any evidence that our love ever existed, but Cassius was Naomi's proof that Wes loved her once. I also started resenting Cassius, just a little bit, but resentment just the same, for the relationship he had with his Dad.

I never went over to Ms. Nola's house on Sunday, so I had no idea that on Sunday they were having family dinners together. I only found out about whose dinners when Ms. Nola invited me to one hoping to end my relationship with her son. Wes usually spent the weekend at his place with Cassius. On Sunday he told me that he dropped Cassius off, but he never told me that he stayed for dinner. Sunday night he told me that he cleaned up his place and sometimes hung out with the fellows, or just chilled at his place. Monday mornings he left for work from his place and spend Monday night through Thursday night with me. As the months went by, I started asking for an occasional Saturday night to go out to dinner, a movie, comedy club to assuage the fear that Cassius would take all of him, leaving nothing for me. How silly I was to think that a father's love for a child was to be compared to the love he had for a woman or that love had a limit? I am still ashamed of how I felt back then.

One Saturday morning we woke up to a heavy downpour. Looking out the window the world seemed wrapped up in a silent gray cocoon. The sun never came out, so the day looked more like early evening instead of the beginning of a new day. Wes and I snuggled in bed most of the morning until hunger won out and he went to go get something to eat. After we ate, I brushed my teeth, showered and put-on sweats, T-shirt and socks. Wes went into the bathroom after I finished. I was laying on the couch when he came out of the bedroom dressed in jeans, T-shirt, tennis shoes and a jacket.

"Where are you going?" I asked.

"I thought I would go and chill with Cassius for a while."

"Oh, okay…but it's raining what can you do with him in the rain?"

"Nothing baby, I'm just going to hang out with him for a little bit. I don't know how long I'm going to be," Wes said as he headed toward the door.

"Hey! Where my kiss?"

Wes turned around and gave me a peck on the lips before walking out the door. I fell asleep on the couch and I woke up to total darkness. It was eerily quiet except for the soft dripping of water running off the eaves. I got up from the sofa and turned on the lights and drew the curtains. I went into the kitchen to check the time on the microwave. It was 10:02 p.m.

"Wes!" I yelled out, even though I could feel the emptiness of the apartment. After looking into the bathroom, and bedroom. I checked the answering machine before I sat back down on the couch and wondered where the hell could Wes be. If Wes was going to spend the night at his place why didn't he say so, or call me if he decided not to come back? I decided to call him instead of sitting here trying to figure it out. No answer, he must be asleep, so I got up from the couch, made myself a sandwich and turned on the TV. After a couple of hours, I decided to go to bed. Wes did not come over the next day, which was Sunday, that was not unusual, but why hadn't he called?

Around 2:00 p.m. I called his number again. No answer, so I called Ms. Nola's house. Ms. Nola answered the phone and informed me that Wes has taken Cassius to MacDonald's. She assured me that she would tell him I called, then she did something I would have never imagined: she invited me to dinner and even invited me to come over early and spend some time with her before dinner. I told her I would be on my way in a couple of hours. I was pleasantly surprised but the feeling that something else was going on had me feeling uneasy. I decided I would go ahead and get myself together for the work week, so I pulled out my clothes that needed to be ironed for the week. I set the ironing board up in the living room in front of the TV and began the relaxing chore of ironing my clothes. As I ironed my clothes, I visualized what blouse I would wear with what pants, as well as what earrings, necklace and shoes. Most people I knew hated ironing, but I enjoyed ironing and planning what I was going to wear for the week instead of getting up in the morning trying to decide what to wear, let alone ironing my clothes each morning. After ironing all the clothes, I needed for the week, I broke down the ironing board and put the board and basket of un-ironed clothes back in the closet and hung up my freshly ironed clothes. I showered, put on jeans, a nice blouse and my beloved brown riding boots.

On the drive to Ms. Nola's house, I knew in the back of my head this was not going to end well, but I had to find out what was going on. I parked in front of Ms. Nola's house but walking to her front door was like playing a game of hopscotch as I tried not to step on the worms that were always on the sidewalk when it rained. I passed Wes's car parked in the driveway and knocked on the front door. Ms. Nola opened the door smiling.

"Why hello dear, come on in," said Ms. Nola.

"Hi, how are you, Ms. Nola."

Cassius was asleep on the couch. Ms. Nola remained standing and smiling at me.

"I'm fine, dear. How are you?"

"I'm good. Where's Wes?" I asked.

"He's in his room," she said raising her hand in the direction I should go. It was something about Ms. Nola's eagerness for me to go into Wes's room that I knew Wes and Naomi were in that room together doing something they could not do in front of Cassius. I froze for a moment and tried to decide if I wanted to know what was going on. I started down the hallway, Ms. Nola stood in the living room where she was sure to see my reaction. I was almost at the door when I heard Naomi making sounds like the ones I made when Wes and I made love. I stopped in front of the door reached for the doorknob, but instead of opening the door I glanced back toward the living room. Ms. Nola was still facing the hallway looking at me, wanting me to open the door. I looked at the door that Wes and Naomi were behind then I walked back into the living room and brushed pass Ms. Nola. I stopped at the front door and looked down at Cassius before opening the door. I looked back at Ms. Nola, she stood in the same spot with one hand on her hip, her lips pulled to one side, turned down looking at me with disgust.

"You have a good night, Ms. Nola. Sorry I can't stay for dinner," I said. Before I could close the door. "You know we have family dinners here every Sunday. Didn't Wes tell you?" hissed Ms. Nola.

Surprisingly, I did not cry on the drive home, instead I was numb. All I could do was think about the last few months and how good it felt to have Wes openly in my life. We were in a relationship; we did more than just sleep with each other. I turned the radio off and cracked the window open. The night sky felt heavy like a blue velvet cloth closing in on me. The atmosphere smelled like another storm was brewing. I breathed deeply, breathing in through my nose, and exhaling out of my mouth. How ironic I thought, our roles had reversed, Naomi was the side chick now.

If Ms. Nola had asked me to step aside and let Wes grieve the loss of his son, as he strengthened his bond with his other son, I might have done that, but it was the way she tried to eliminate me that made me refuse to leave.

The next day was Monday. I went to work and came home like nothing had happened. Around 6:30 p.m. Wes let himself into the apartment; dinner was ready, and we ate, watched TV, went to bed, made love, went to sleep, woke up and started the day all over again. I would catch myself looking at Wes for some sign of guilt, some trace of remorse; if I did not know that he had slept with Naomi, I would not have known it by his actions. The week went by pretty much as all the other weeks, except I knew my life with Wes was perfidious.

Our whole relationship had been one or the other of us walking away and coming back, but never had we both let go at the same time. That should have been the time that we both let go, but I did not want Naomi to win. My hatred of Ms. Nola and Naomi began the night that Ms. Nola invited me to dinner.

During that period in our relationship, when I knew Wes had slept with Naomi, I would wake up in the middle of the night wondering if he would come back Monday. I would check the closet Friday when I got home from work to make sure his clothes were still there, I would check the bathroom to see if his toothbrush, razor and colognes were there, then I would breathe easier until I wondered if he was with Naomi. I knew he was capable of love because he loved his son and his mother, and if asked I would have said he loved me.

Ms. Nola's behavior that Sunday helped me to nurture the delusion that Wes was the victim in a plot Naomi and Ms. Nola cooked up to break us up. Wes succumbed to Naomi's seductions that one time and that was it. Somehow, I could live with that, so I slipped on my rose-colored lenses that I never took off, not even to sleep. How could I? I needed the illusion of the ethereal world they created to cuddle up with and lull myself to sleep.

My hatred for Naomi and Ms. Nola began to grow. Every day I replayed offenses or slights committed by Ms. Nola or Naomi in my head. I remembered the times Naomi called my house and demanded to speak with Wes because their son wanted to speak with his Dad, or how Ms. Nola never said hello to me when I answered the phone and did not ask me to call her Mom, but Naomi called her Mom ad nauseam in my presence. Wes never knew how much I hated his Mother and Naomi.

I began to plot and scheme how I could insert myself in Wes's visits with Cassius. I began making suggestions and eventually started going on the Saturday outings, so I would be in the car when Wes picked up Cassius at Ms. Nola's house. The days that Ms. Nola or Naomi would be outside watering the grass or sitting on the porch when Wes and I pulled up to pick up Cassius were the best. We would exchange greetings with fake smiles on our faces, as long as, Wes was within earshot or could see us; if not, we would just mean mug each other.

On the nights when I was all alone and I could not sleep, the rose-colored lenses would slip, and I would catch a glimpse of the woman I had become. I had become a woman who lived in the shadow of a man that was not honest with her. I was a woman who was afraid to know the truth and slunk in the shadows careful not to make a sound. On those sleepless nights I focused my thoughts on the two people I blamed for the shadows I lived in instead of removing the rose- colored lenses and face the truth.

Chapter 4

"Babe, what are we going to do for Thanksgiving?" I asked.

"You're not going to your parents?" asked Wes getting up from the couch and coming into the kitchen.

"I thought I would spend Thanksgiving with you at your Mom's house. Don't you want to spend Thanksgiving together?"

"Yeah, babe, but I thought you were spending Thanksgiving with your parents," said Wes, as he hugged me from behind, and started kissing my neck while I was sautéing the chicken. I shrugged him off and told him, I would be spending Christmas with my parents.

"That's not cool. Don't miss Thanksgiving with your parents on my account." Wes rested, his chin on my shoulder, so I hunched my shoulder and dislodged him.

"Don't worry about it, they're okay with me missing Thanksgiving this year---oh, and they can't wait to meet you." I said turning slightly toward him with a big fake smile on my face. Wes straightened himself up, pasted a half smile on his face as he realized that his attempt to change my mind had failed. Wes went back to the living room sat on the couch and watched the game as I prepared dinner.

Thanksgiving was a week away, so after dinner I called Ms. Nola and asked what I should bring for Thanksgiving, making sure Wes could hear me.

"You don't have to bring nothing. Matter of fact don't bring yourself," chuckled Ms. Nola.

"Not on your life, Ms. Nola, I'll bring a peach cobbler. Is that okay?" I asked a dead phone line.

Wes looked up from the couch—I would have sworn that I saw a bead of perspiration on his forehead—and then he looked back at the TV. I was so impressed with myself that I sat next to him and started talking about what to get Cassius and Ms. Nola for Christmas.

Mom and Dad were disappointed that I would not make it for Thanksgiving but were looking forward to my visit at Christmas. I was like a kid on Christmas Eve, I could not wait for Thanksgiving Day. Finally, Thanksgiving Day arrived, and I woke early so I could bake my peach cobbler. By the time Wes got up, I was taking the cobbler out of the oven. It looked perfect. I had baked the cobbler with little squares of dough baked inside and had placed a latticed crust on top with cut outs of leaves scattered artistically on the top. Wes did not look too good that morning; he slow dragged all morning. The peach cobbler was wrapped in foil on the counter, I was in the shower when Wes joined me. I knew exactly what he was doing, I guess he thought I would opt to stay in bed with him instead of going to his mother's house for Thanksgiving. After Wes's performance in the shower my resolve weakened a little, nothing would have been better than to spend the rest of the day in bed, but the thought of him and Naomi gave me the motivation to get dressed. On the way to Ms. Nola's house, Wes held my hand while he was driving, that was different because he never wanted to hold hands, especially if he was driving. I had always initiated the hand holding. Wes pulled into Ms. Nola's driveway and got out of the car not bothering to open the door for me or retrieve the cobbler in the back seat. I got out of the car and got the cobbler from the back of the car as Wes waited for me on the porch, when I got close to the front door, he opened it for me, and we walked in together.

"Why is it so hot in here?" asked Wes.

"Because we're cooking in here," laughed Naomi. Her smile drooped when she saw me.

"Everything smells good," I said as I walked pass her to go to the kitchen.

Ms. Nola and Ms. Beulah were in the kitchen sitting at the table.

"About time," barked Ms. Nola. "I thought my turkey wasn't gonna make it. Naomi!" yelled Ms. Nola.

"Hi, Ms. Nola, Ms. Beulah. Happy Thanksgiving," I chirped.

"Happy Thanksgiving, Baby. How you doing?" replied Ms. Beulah.

No acknowledgment from Ms. Nola. Naomi walked into the kitchen and Ms. Nola told her to finish putting everything on the dining table and the serving buffet.

Naomi began putting the food in their serving dishes and placing them on the dining table and buffet, so I began to help without being invited. Wes helped Naomi put the turkey on the platter and he carried it to the dining room table. The buffet was the dessert station while the table held all the main courses. The table was lovely; it was covered with a hand-made lace tablecloth. The food was placed in matching fine bone china with a delicate rose pattern much like my mother's china.

For a moment I missed not being at my mother's house enveloped in my parents' love; how disappointed they must have been to not have me there. Instead, I was here with people who did not want me there. Dinner was a little strained to say the least. Ms. Beulah, God bless her, tried to make things feel normal. Cassius and Ms. Beulah made dinner bearable. Ms. Beulah kept a steady stream of conversation going, and Cassius just being there brought lightness to the room. After dinner Naomi and I cleared the table, and washed and put the dishes up, while Wes, Cassius, Ms. Nola and Ms. Beulah watched TV in the living room.

From the kitchen I could hear laughter and chants from the adults encouraging Cassius to dance. Naomi said she would finish in the kitchen, so I went into the living room and sat in one of the chairs leaving room for Naomi on the couch next to Ms. Nola. After a while I asked if anyone wanted dessert and Wes said he would take some of my peach cobbler with ice cream if there was any ice cream. Ms. Nola said there was, and I got up to get the cobbler and ice cream and asked if anyone else wanted anything. Ms. Beulah wanted a piece of pound cake and Ms. Nola declined dessert. I got Ms. Beulah her piece of cake and gave it to her, I got Wes's peach cobbler from the buffet and walked into the kitchen with his bowl of cobbler to put the ice cream on top when I noticed Naomi washing dishes with her belly pressed against the sink. My eyes noticed something amiss, but my mind did not register what my eyes had seen, not until I handed Wes his cobbler. My vision was blurred from the tears that were flowing down my face.

"Babe, what's wrong?" asked Wes.

"I'm in so much pain. It hurts, it hurts, it hurts," was all I could say.

"What hurts?" asked Wes.

I stumbled to sit down and lowered my head to my feet rocking back and forward chanting it hurts, it hurts. . .

Wes got up and pulled me into his arms. Naomi came out of the kitchen and stood in the dining room and looked at us. Ms. Nola. Ms. Beulah got up from the couch. Ms. Nola asked her son what was wrong with me, Wes shrugged his shoulders and told them that he is going to take me home. Ms. Beulah got my coat and purse and walked with us to the car. Wes put me in the car, Ms. Beulah handed him my coat and purse as he went around to the driver's side. Ms. Nola was standing next to the driver side of the car by the time Wes got into the car and leaned down to the window and asked her son if I was crazy.

When Wes pulled out of the driveway I started screaming at the top of my lungs, by the time we made it to my apartment I was physically and emotionally drained. Wes helped me to my apartment door; a bystander would have thought he was helping a drunk walk, but I was not drunk, I was a wounded thing crawling to shelter to either recover or die. That night I lay in bed in the dark awake, Wes lay next to me and I could feel him watching me. He kept asking me what was wrong, but I could not answer him, because I was trying to find the little girl that sat on the curb smelling the grass and enjoying the sun on her face. Where did she go?

I found myself walking down a dark dirt road. I was not afraid because there was something familiar about the road. I was sure I had travelled it before. It was a road that was beautiful during the day but was ominous in the dark. I could hear rustling in the bushes on the side of the road; something big was moving beside me. As soon as I came to a fork in the road, one path appeared to disappear because it was completely void of light, the other path although dark had a pin prick of light at the end of the road. I stood there looking at the two paths trying to decide which path to take. The path with the light seemed too long to travel, so I stepped onto the path void of light. I shivered and reached for the covers which I had tossed aside earlier, rolled over to my side facing away from Wes and went to sleep. I knew when I rolled over to go to sleep that I had not been dreaming, my mind was teetering over the edge, I was descending into madness and if I continued down the path I chose, there would be no coming back.

The next morning a coldness had encamped around me. Wes tried to talk to me about yesterday, but I did not want to talk about it. I just sat in bed staring at the walls. I was so tired of living this lie. I felt as if I had given up everything to be with Wes and had got nothing in return. Time and time again he betrayed me. I lost so many years, and for what? Something that I was so willing to fight for yesterday was something that I could not stand to have near me now. The coldness that circled around me slowly, insidiously, crawled inside me and replaced the pain that once burned so hot in me, leaving a hollowness instead. Just before the sun set, the time of day that bathed everything in a golden glow I got out of bed and walked into the living room. Wes was on the phone and when he saw me, he quickly hung up.

"Hey, babe. Are you feeling better?"

"Not really."

"Do you want something to eat?"

"No."

"What's wrong, baby?"

"Naomi pregnant, that's what's wrong."

"Baby, what are you talking about? Did Naomi tell you she was pregnant?"

"I saw her stomach yesterday when she was washing dishes. What, she hasn't told you yet?"

"Why would she tell me she's pregnant?"

"Really, Wes? You're going to sit here and tell me that you haven't been fucking her?"

"Who told you some shit like that?"

"Nobody had to tell me. I fucking heard you guys! Oh, you didn't know that your mother invited me to one of your Sunday dinners. I heard you!" I screamed.

Wes sputtered but did not say anything that I could understand.

"Why, Wes, why do you keep hurting me?"

"I didn't mean to hurt you."

"You didn't think fucking Naomi would hurt me?"

"Come on, man, it just happened."

"Why did you call me when Wesley Jr. died? Why me and not Naomi? Was it because I was closer, or you knew my weak ass would jump at a chance to be with you?"

"Don't do that. You know why I called you. I needed you Eloise."

"If you need me so bad, then why do you keep fucking other people? If you need me, why did you let me kill our baby?"

Wes just stood there deflated before me, his shoulder slumped down.

"You don't need me; you just use me. What's wrong with me? Why can't you love me?" I shouted.

Wes gave up trying to respond to me. He walked over to me and pulled me to him and held on to me. Wes tilted my chin with his hand forcing me to look at his face. He held my gaze assessing me, trying to determine if the truth would do me more harm than good before he answered.

"This is who I am. I don't know why I do the things I do. Maybe this is all I know. Niggas fuck around. You want to know why I want you? It's because it feels good fucking you, period! I don't have to leave, but your pride won't let me stay, and you shouldn't let me stay because I'll probably fuck up again. I want you when I want you, Eloise, and I still want to do what I want to do. I'm not ready to settle down. Naomi knows that, but she knows I'm going to be there for my kids, because I want them to know me."

I tried to pull away from Wes, but he held on even tighter. I could not look him in his eyes because I knew he was telling the truth.

Wes kissed me deep and hard. We both knew in that moment he could have had me, but for some reason he took mercy on me, released me and walked out the door. I watched him walk out the door, almost calling him back, almost surrendering to that weak crazed woman that came so close to the surface she almost took me with her into the abyss.

Chapter 5

Christmas came and went without me putting up one Christmas decoration, I did not participate in any of the courthouse holiday events, but I did go to visit my parents for Christmas. I forced myself to smile and laugh when it was expected, and I tried to hide the sadness that threatened to overtake me. One night I was walking down the stairs and I saw my Mom hand my Dad a plate with a big wedge of lemon meringue pie.

"I thought there was no more pie left," said Dad.

"I hid this for you; I know it's your favorite," said Mom.

"Thanks, chicken," said Dad before putting a big piece of pie into his mouth while smiling at my Mom.

Mom sat on the couch next to her rooster reading a book, while he watched TV and ate his pie. As I was watching them it occurred to me that, that was how love expressed itself. My Mom was always thinking about my Dad, it occurred to me then, that Wes was thinking about me when he walked out. He could have stayed, I would have let him, but he knew it would have been a matter of time before he broke me. I felt myself slipping away and becoming someone else, Wes saw a glimpse of that someone else as he walked me out his mother's house Thanksgiving Day. Ms. Nola saw it as well, and for a moment even she was scared.

Since this was my last day with Mom and Dad. Mom and I decided to take down the Christmas decorations. Dad was upstairs taking a nap and Mom and I were taking the ornaments off the small Christmas tree.

"Baby! are you okay?" asked my Mom out of the blue.

"Yeah, I'm good, why?"

"I don't know. You just seem kinda sad. Is everything okay?"

"I'm good, Mom. I just broke up with this guy I was seeing. You know, the one I spent Thanksgiving with."

"Ah, baby. I'm so sorry it didn't work out. You don't think you and Wes will get back together?"

"Naw, I don't think so," I said as I bent over and put glass ornaments back into their boxes.

"Give it some time. You guys might be able to work it out."

"I don't think so."

"Do you want to talk about it? Mom, asked, and before I could respond, "Maybe it will make you feel better." She added.

"Naw, I don't feel like talking about it." I responded.

"You'll find somebody one day, or better yet, he'll find you."

Five years had passed since I last saw Wes. He did not call me, and I did not call him. I was getting older, but I was still young enough to turn heads when I tried. I was not really seeing anyone, but I did have a friend with benefits. My problem was I compared everyone to Wes. Nobody was Wes, so I stopped trying to find that somebody, instead I hooked up with my friend with benefits, Michael, whenever I felt the need. Funny how my emotions did not get mixed up with what my body needed from Michael. Michael was a tall chocolate brother with broad shoulders, cut abs and powerful thighs. The only thing Michael was lacking was intelligence. While he could stimulate my body, I could hardly wait for him to satisfy me and get out. Trust me you did not want to watch "Jeopardy" with him. The emotional detachment that I had with Michael gave me a better understanding of the relationship I had with Wes. I found a kind of peace knowing that the hurt I felt was not an intentional wounding. Michael was a toy that I could pick up and put down whenever I got bored, and if he got hurt that had more to do with him than me, and the same was true for me and Wes. Wes taught me to guard my heart, and that sex was not personal, it was just a function of the body, one of many functions that the body performed. He also taught me about love, however inadvertently it may have been. He taught me that love involved the essence of your whole being.

Because I had not gotten married and I did not have a kid, the number of girlfriends in my life dwindled. Married women did not want a single girl hanging around their husbands. I was down to one girlfriend who found herself in the same boat that I was in—single and no steady man. Gina was something else, she was wild and fun to be around. She attracted both men and women wherever she went. She was the one woman I knew who could successfully have casual sex without the niceties of feeling. She would ask a man to leave her bed or she would leave if he failed to produce an orgasm. She had gone to a man's place, had sex, and left because she was satisfied and wanted to watch the News in her own bed alone eating ice cream. How she got away with her shenanigans was beyond me, but when she was done with whoever was the flavor of the month they parted on good terms and considered her a friend. Gina's petite frame was always tightly clad and because she was only 5 feet 2 inches, I had never seen her in flats. She was a Court Clerk like me, and we worked in the same courthouse. Back in the day Gina was messing around with a married bailiff who she dropped to become this white married attorney's mistress. The difference between the bailiff and attorney was, the bailiff was getting it for free and the attorney was paying for it. Gina never told me the attorney's name because she did not want to mess up her good thing. This nameless attorney was a partner at a prestigious law firm and saw Gina in court during a trial. After a few court appearances on his case, he asked Gina to lunch. He took her to the Los Angeles Athletic Club, a private elite club in downtown Los Angeles. After lunch he took her to his office and showed her the pictures on his desk of his wife and children and propositioned her. The proposition was, and I quote: "I'm married, and I will never leave my wife and kids. I make a lot of money, and I will buy you whatever you want, I just want to fuck you." To which Gina said hell yeah!

Gina and I began to party hearty on her Sugar Daddy's money. I felt like her pimp because of the perks I got from their relationship. I was the third wheel in their affair. I would have dinner or drinks with Gina at downtown hotels while she waited for Nameless to finish a business meeting. There was a time when he was hearing a long-cause class action civil trial and his firm put him up at a downtown hotel, which was closer to the courthouse then his office, and he put Gina up in a suite, so he could slip in and out. It was on one of those nights that Gina and I had finished dinner and were chilling on the rooftop of the hotel having drinks when I saw Wes and Melvin drinking at the bar. Melvin was scanning the rooftop when he noticed me and gave me the chin up nod and nudged Wes. Wes looked at Melvin and Melvin must have told him to look in my direction because he looked in my direction scanning the area until he found me. Wes and Melvin walked over and sat across from us. Melvin was grinning and eyeballing Gina. I introduced Gina to Wes and Melvin.

"So how do you know my girl Eloise?" asked Gina.

"We used to kick it back in the day," said Wes.

"Oh, ooh, yeah so you that nigga?"

"Yeah, I'm that nigga," replied Wes looking directly at me.

"Come on man, with that shit. This is a new day. You're looking good Gina. Why don't you come chill with me and let these two catch up? What you drinking?"

Melvin stood up, assuming Gina was going to take him up on the offer. Gina blew air out her mouth, dismissing Melvin.

"My man will be here any minute and I don't think he would be too pleased to see me having a drink with you."

"Oh, it's like that."

"It's exactly like that," said Gina as she uncrossed and recrossed her legs.

Melvin made a blanket declaration of moving on to greener pastures and walked back to the bar. Wes stated it was nice seeing me and meeting Gina after which he got up and joined Melvin at the bar. A few minutes later, Nameless appeared and signaled to Gina. Gina hugged me before she got up to follow Nameless to the elevator. I sat there enjoying the warm night and my cocktail. I looked toward the bar and caught Wes looking at me. I turned away from him and closed my eyes and tried to deal with all the emotions that invaded my mind and body. When I opened my eyes, Wes was seated across from me watching me as if I was his prey. We sat there for what felt like a long time not saying anything just looking and waiting for the other one to make the first move. Finally, Melvin came over and plopped down in the seat next to Wes.

"Man, you ready to leave?" asked Melvin.

"Naw, man I'm good. I'll see you tomorrow."

"Nigga, I rode with you."

Wes stood up and fished in his pocket for his keys and gave them to Melvin.

"I'm going to get me a room, man, so pick me up in the morning."

"Alright, nigga," Melvin looked at Wes, then at me grinning like the Cheshire Cat before leaving.

"You still with Naomi?" I asked.

"Yes."

"She lets you stay out all night?"

"She's out of town visiting her parents. Your man let you stay out all night?"

"He wouldn't if I had a man."

"Would you like to have a drink with me in my room?"

"You don't have a room."

"Well, if I get a room, would you have a drink with me in my room?"

"I don't know," I said, trying to see if he was still the man that told me that he was gonna do what he wanted to do. Wes got up to go get the room. I watched him walk across the bar to the elevator. I wondered how many side chicks he had, and I knew as I watched him get into the elevator that I would be having drinks and more in his room. I knew before I stood up to meet him in the lobby that I could not just dip my toes in his waters; I knew I would submerge my whole being in him and it was a good possibility that I would get hurt again, but I did not want to keep walking around numb, waiting for something, anything to happen. So, I finished my drink and got up to meet Wes in the lobby.

That night Wes and I made love all night and just like the first night I closed my eyes and refused to think about Naomi or the kids. I did not worry about the consequences; I did not care. All I knew was that I was going to hold on to Wes for as long as possible. This time I knew going in that nothing would change, that Wes would not leave his family. I knew I was the one that would be left lying on the ground broken, and still I dove into his waters headfirst, feeling so light, so free. I had left my heart unguarded, I was already losing control.

During the night, in between lovemaking, Wes told me that he and Naomi got married about a year ago, and their second child was another boy. He told me straight out that nothing had changed, he would not leave Naomi and his kids, so it was all up to me if we were going to do this thing or not. I told him that I knew he would not leave his kids, and that all I wanted was him, anyway I could have him. As I lay in Wes's arm that night, I felt like we were the only two people in the world, and for the moment we were. I relaxed my mind and body in our dark isolated world.

That night we talked about what had been going on in our lives since the last time we were together. I eventually told him about Gina, and her situation, which was why I was there that night. He got real interested in

Nameless. He asked if he liked to party because he knew how those white boys like to do coke and he could supply him with almost anything that he might need. He asked me to check with Gina and let him know. The next morning Wes gave me his pager number, and I gave him my home number. I knew there were only two types of people that carried pagers, doctors and drug dealers.

"Are you still working for the city?"

"Yeah, why?" asked Wes.

"Then why do you have a pager?"

"It's a little something I do to make ends meet."

"Wes, you're not selling crack. Please, tell me you're not selling crack."

"Naw, I'm not selling crack. I wouldn't have a job if I was selling that shit. I wouldn't be able to make it from my front door to the car without crack heads running up on me. I sell mostly weed, cocaine and X. I do the clubs, private parties and occasionally a rave."

"You at a rave?" I said smiling at the thought of Wes at a rave.

"Not if I can help it, but I can come up at a rave," said Wes laughing. "Besides, I don't feel bad when I sell to privileged white kids."

The fact that Wes was now married to Naomi with two kids and selling drugs should have stopped me, but it did not because I too wanted to be like my friend Gina. I wanted to take what I wanted without any consequences.

Wes and I started off strong like always, I expected it to peter out like before, but it did not, Wes was working me like he was working a job and before I knew it, I was strung again. I did anything and everything Wes asked me to do. When I asked Gina if she and Nameless did any drugs, she told me that they did coke, and how he sprinkled cocaine on her body when they got down. I told her that Wes said he could hook Nameless up if he needed anything. Soon Wes and I began partying with Gina and Nameless. Wes and Melvin began supplying other Westside attorneys and their clients with their drug of choice. Everybody was happy. Wes was happy because he and Melvin picked up a lot of new clients; Gina and I were happy because both our men were showing us a good time and spending a lot of money on us.

Everything was going good until one day Nameless needed Gina to file an Answer to a class action civil case. When Gina told him, Clerks did not file Answers in the courtroom, he told her that he knew that, but he needed her to file the document for him and back date it because his firm did not answer the complaint in a timely manner, and this could possibly cost them millions. Gina was afraid to do what Nameless was asking and wanted me to help her. We decided that we would go to work on Saturday when there would only be a few people around.

Gina had pulled the case file from the file room during the week and locked the file in her file cabinet in her courtroom. Nameless had given her the document he needed filed as well as two copies to file as confirmed copies. Gina and I worked on our backlogs. After a couple of hours, I met her in her department, and we walked down to the civil clerk's office. There were a few people that we did not really know milling around until one of the guys there started talking about going to get something to eat. While they were huddled around that person's desk, Gina and I walked past a desk and picked up a file stamp. After we got back to Gina's department, we filed the Answer to the Complaint with someone else's file stamp, which had that person's name on it. We put the original filed document in the case file, took the file back to the file room, and put the file stamp back on the desk we took it from.

Gina and I hung out downtown for the rest of the day until Nameless could meet us. We had just finished a late lunch when he came into the restaurant. He sat next to Gina and across from me as if it was a business meeting. We greeted each other and Gina passed him the manila envelope with the confirmed copies and Nameless passed an envelope to Gina and then he passed me an envelope.

"What's this?" I asked.

"Just something to show my appreciation. I can't stay, but you ladies enjoy yourself," said Nameless as he got up to leave.

Gina peeked inside her envelope and smiled. I put my envelope in my purse without looking. I was trying to be cool, but I was nervous and ready to leave. Once I got into the car, I counted the money in the envelope—twenty thousand dollars. That is when I told myself that with this money and the money Wes occasionally gave me for hooking him up with Nameless and his connections, I was going to buy a house. If I could not have the family, I was going to have the house and the white picket fence.

Chapter 6

The day I closed escrow on my first house, I called Wes. We made plans to move me in at the end of the month. I had begun packing up my apartment when I opened escrow so there was not a lot left to pack. Saturday could not roll around quick enough for me. When Saturday finally came, I was up early waiting for Wes to get there with the moving truck. We made quick work of packing me up. I stopped by the manager's apartment and gave him the key and my new address where he could send me my security deposit.

Wes and I could not stop smiling as we unpacked the moving van. The utilities were turned on, but the refrigerator was being delivered Monday. The sellers sold me their vintage stove for a good price, because it weighed a ton, and they did not want to move it. Wes and I blessed the living room by making love on the floor surrounded by boxes. After the bed was delivered, we christened the bed too, after which Wes said he had to go and return the truck.

"Wait a minute," I said as I rummaged through my purse. I smiled and stretched out my hand.

"This is for you. This is our home," I said as I placed a house key in his hand.

Wes kissed me on the lips and then kissed me on my forehead and patted me on my back. I thought he was being condescending because I always felt that way when someone patted my back, I was about to shrug his hand off my back when I looked up at him and saw the look on his face. I had given him something that he did not expect, and I believed then, and will always believe that he cherished that house as much as I did.

"You better go before you get something started," I teased.

Our home, as I called it, was soon furnished with new pieces and old pieces I picked up at thrift stores and yard sales. I loved old furniture. My living room had a new brown velvet sofa, a glass coffee table that rested on a beautiful rug with an Ikat design featuring rust, brown and cream. The large wicker basket containing my Ficus tree was in the corner of the living room by the large front window, an antique pine console table ran alongside the wall opposite the sofa and near the front door providing you a place to set your keys and anything you had in your hands when you entered the house. And on the last wall of the living room was a vintage 1950s blonde oak china cabinet. The top of the cabinet had two shelves and glass doors which contained crystal decanters, liquor and glasses; the bottom part of the cabinet was closed storage.

The kitchen had an old fashion banquette, which I loved and the O'Keefe and Merritt stove that the previous owner sold me. The kitchen cabinets were original to the house and even had a pull-out cutting board and a peninsula which contained display shelves at the end. The house had three bedrooms and two bathrooms. The largest bedroom I took as my own, and one of the bedrooms I set up as a guest room, and the other bedroom became the den. In the den I had the closet doors removed and converted the closet into built-in bookshelves with a large opening in the middle to house the television and closed storage at the bottom.

The backyard was large and in need of a gardener's touch. The first few months Wes and I worked on the yard; we trimmed hedges and edged up the flower beds. Every weekend for months I was either in the yard or painting old furniture. I loved my house and enjoyed arranging and rear-ranging the furniture and my knickknacks. Mom and Dad drove down and spent a week with me in the summer. They were very, impressed with the house. Wes even came over one night and had dinner with us. When Dad asked Wes what he did for a living and what he felt about settling down and having a family, I held my breath until Wes said he worked for the city and family was very, important to him. Wes looked over at me and winked. Mom was totally taken with Wes and was quick to tell me that things had a way of working out. Mom had remembered Wes as the boy I broke up with just before Christmas a few years ago.

After Wes left that night my Dad went around looking at the house again and he wandered into my bedroom. While he was in there, I heard my closet door open and close. When I asked my Dad what he was looking for, he told me he was looking to see if there were any men clothes in my closet. Mom and I laughed, and I assured my father that Wes did not live with me. What would my father say if he knew that Wes was married with kids?

My house soon became the party spot. Wes and I threw barbeques constantly during the summer. When we did have people over, Wes would spend the night. What he told Naomi on the nights that he did not come home I never knew, nor did I care; I just savored the time we spent together. At one of our weekend get-togethers, Wes, Gina, Melvin and I were sitting in the backyard drinking and listening to music. Gina went into the house to get herself something to eat. Shortly after, Melvin went into the house to get himself something to eat, too. At the end of the song that was playing Wes asked how long that had been going on.

"What?"

"How long has Melvin and Gina been fucking around?"

"What makes you think that?"

"Eloise, how long does it take to make a plate?" Wes asked and looked over at me and wiggled his eyebrows up and down. Wes and I finished our drink and decided to call it a night. After we picked up the debris and turned off the lights in the backyard, we went into the house through the kitchen door.

"Where's everybody?" asked Wes, smiling.

We put our glasses into the sink, and I walked down the hall to the den—no Gina or Melvin. So, I tiptoed to the guest bedroom and listened at the door. Yep, they were in there. I sneaked back to our bedroom where Wes was undressing.

"They're in the guest room," I whispered. Wes laughed and asked why was I whispering?

"Come here," Wes said and pulled me to him. Wes began to undress me, and I did not think about Gina or Melvin until the next morning.

The next morning, I got up to make coffee. I went to the guest room door and lightly tapped on the door.

"Yes," said Gina.

"Do you guys want breakfast?"

"Yeah," said Melvin. Gina giggled.

I put a full pot of coffee on then went back into my bedroom, where I brushed my teeth and took a quick shower and dressed. Wes stumbled out of the bed and asked why I was getting dressed. I told him Melvin and Gina were still here and I was going to make breakfast.

"Oh," said Wes and went into the bathroom.

After breakfast was ready and we were sitting at the kitchen ban-quette eating breakfast, Melvin suggested that we ride up to Las Vegas for the day. Wes agreed, and Gina said she needed to go home first to change her clothes. Melvin rode with Gina, and Wes and I followed in his car to her apartment. We went up to Gina's apartment to wait for her to shower and change. Melvin went into her bedroom to shower and put back on his same clothes.

Wes and I were sitting on the couch watching TV, waiting for Melvin and Gina when Wes got impatient and started banging on Gina's bedroom door, telling them to come on. Melvin peeped his head out the door and told Wes there had been a change of plan. Wes told Melvin that he was going to spend another night with me and that he would pick him up tomorrow afternoon. Wes whispered to Melvin, that if Naomi asked to tell her there was a hold up in picking up the stuff. So, that was what he told Naomi on the nights he did not go home. I wondered to myself if Naomi was now the one wearing glasses with rose-colored lenses. How would she feel if she found out that Wes was still messing around with me? Naomi and Ms. Nola had won the game that we played back when Wes and I were together, but Naomi was paying a heavy price for her happiness now. She must stay awake at night wondering just as I did if he was with someone else when he came home late or not at all.

Monday, Gina and I had lunch, and I asked Gina what was going on with Melvin.

"Gurrl, I was drunk, and Melvin was looking good, so I decided to give it a whirl. And damn, girl, it was good."

"What about Nameless?"

"What about Nameless? Ain't nothing changed. Nameless got a wife, and Melvin is…well, you know Melvin. So now I got me a sugar daddy and some good dick," laughed Gina.

"Gurl, you're crazy."

Gina continued to see Nameless and Melvin, and I continued to see Wes. It was good until Melvin almost messed up Gina's good thing. We were partying at one of Nameless client's parties in the Hollywood Hills. Wes and Melvin were making good money at the party selling drugs to rich people bored with their financially stable lives, looking for something new and exciting. Melvin was getting more and more agitated watching Gina get high off coke and hanging all over Nameless. Melvin walked over to Gina and Nameless and started pulling on Gina. Nameless had just bent over to snort a line of coke, Gina bumped Nameless while pulling away from Melvin. By the time Nameless had finished his line and was looking up to see what was going on I bumped into him on the opposite side, almost spilling the rest of his coke. As I was apologizing and helping him with his mirror full of coke, Wes pulled Melvin off Gina, and walked him outside.

"What's wrong with you, nigga?" Wes hissed.

"I'm tired of that white motherfucker slobbering all over my bitch."

"Come on man, you know that motherfucker gives us plenty of business. We're leaving money on the table if we leave now, so can you handle it, or do we need to go before you fuck our shit up?"

"I'm good, I'm good, man, come on let's go get that money," said Melvin.

Wes let Melvin go, and Melvin hunched his shoulders a couple of times before they went back into the party. Gina and Nameless were in the bathroom doing God knows what when Wes and Melvin came back into the house. Wes whispered in my ear that they were going to circulate the party until they were sold out. I told him OK, and that I would wait for them here.

When Gina and Nameless stumbled out of the bathroom, Nameless walked Gina over to me and said he would be leaving soon. He left Gina with me and proceeded to work the party, shaking hands, patting people on the back, and he even called Melvin over to facilitate a drug transaction before he left. When Wes and Melvin were finished with their business they came and got us. On the ride home Melvin was going off on Gina in the back seat, and Gina was cussing him out. When we got to Gina's apartment Wes asked Melvin if he was staying with Gina or coming with us.

"I'm good man. Pick me up tomorrow," said Melvin as he got out of the car with Gina.

That was our lives until it was not, Wes, Melvin, Gina and I went on for years like that—sex, drugs and rock and roll. Technology even conspired with us to make cheating and lying easier. Wes and Melvin traded in their pagers for cell phones. Cellphones and personal computers had started becoming more and more commonplace. Soon we began dabbling with chat rooms such as Black Planet. Myspace came on the scene, and before we could get used to My Space, a thing call Facebook changed the game. Everyone was running around trying to get more friends than the next person, and soon I was able to see what my nemesis, Naomi, was up to.

Naomi's life on Facebook was picture perfect. Naomi used Facebook like it was her personal diary with the added bonus of pictures. In the beginning I would go to Melvin's Facebook page just to see what Wes was doing on his birthday, on holidays, on the days he could not spend with me, or if there were longer periods of time between his visits. I was able to see Naomi's post because she was friends with Melvin. I never posted anything I just watched Naomi's life from the privacy of my home. The transition between occasionally looking at Naomi's posts and daily looking at Naomi's posts kind of snuck up on me before I realized that I was doing it.

Once it dawned on me that I was obsessing and seeing how it affected me, I tried to not look at it every day. When that failed, I decided that I would not look at it until the end of the day when I was home alone. I would come home from work, and before I could get out of my work clothes, I would sit in front of the computer strolling down Melvin's page looking for Naomi's post. Sometimes I thought she posted pictures of her and Wes for my benefit. Wes's eyes smiling into the camera looked directly at me. He seemed happy with his wife, there was an easy casualness in the way they touched each other in the photographs that were obviously taken spontaneously; even the pictures that they posed for emitted an historic intimacy. Wes had never told me he was unhappy at home, only that he would not leave because of the kids. Looking at Naomi's post only made me want what they had, I wanted to be the one standing in front of the camera smiling as he draped his arms around me.

Chapter 7

"Gurrl, Nameless rented a house for the weekend in Palm Springs. His firm is having a conference in Palm Springs and he wants us to spend some time together before he goes back home," said Gina.

"Is Melvin going to be cool with you going away for the weekend?"

"Melvin ain't my man, so he ain't got shit to say about it," replied Gina.

"Oh, so you haven't mentioned it to him?"

"Nope, because it's none of his business," hissed Gina

"OK, so when I talk to Wes should I tell him about Nameless or not."

"Wes don't need to know my business neither," said Gina sheepishly looking in my direction.

"OK, so I'll just tell him you and I are having a girl's weekend in Palm Springs."

We sat for a few minutes eating our lunch lost in our own thoughts. I could not understand how Gina could continue her relationship with Nameless since she and Melvin were together all the time. I ended my friends with benefit relationship with Michael when Wes and I got back together again, because everything I had to give was for Wes.

"Would you give up Nameless for Melvin?" I asked more for something to say because the silence had gone on too long.

"Yeah, I would, if he gave up his women for me," Gina stopped and looked thoughtful, her face softened. "Guys have always wanted only one thing from me. That's why I said yes to Nameless. He was honest and straight up with me; with him I went into this situation with my eyes wide opened and with no expectations. Melvin caught me by surprise, I didn't expect to like him as much as I do. I want all of him and I want him to want all of me, but if I can't have it that way then I'm going to keep it moving."

That weekend in Palm Springs was amazing. Gina and I would get up in the morning and have our breakfast and coffee by the pool before it got too hot. We would go to all the thrift stores in Palm Springs and the surrounding area, then have lunch, go back to the house and take a nap. We would go out to dinner, come back and have drinks by the pool. Nameless would come over and Gina would go and entertain him. After he would leave, Gina and I would laugh, talk, drink and listen to music by the pool.

On the way back home Melvin was blowing up Gina's phone. When we got to Gina's apartment Melvin was there waiting for her, but I did not find that out until Monday at lunch. When I got to Gina's apartment we hugged and said goodbye at her carport where my car was parked. Monday at lunch Gina told me that Melvin had moved in with her, and she and Nameless were done.

"Does Nameless know that?" I asked.

"Not yet, but he won't care. He'll just go and get someone else to fuck him," Gina laughed.

My friend was happy, and I was happy for her. Gina did the one thing I had been trying to do for years. For the rest of the lunch Gina talked about Melvin this and Melvin that. Gina was saying his name as often as she could because like all women in love, she liked the sound of his name as it floated around in the atmosphere and the feel of his name as it tickled her tongue. After lunch we walked back to my courtroom. I was blinking back tears, not wanting Gina to see. Once again, I was wishing I were in another woman's shoes.

How many years had I been stuck in this place with Wes, wanting something that I knew I could never have. I could not understand why

Gina and Melvin's relationship did not give me hope that maybe, just maybe, Wes would choose me, but it did not. Instead it made me more hopeless. I knew in my heart that Wes was never going to choose me, he would not have slept with Naomi and conceived a second child with her. I should have known it when he got Shapira pregnant and chose her over me. Wes used his kids as an excuse not to have a life with me, so while I called Naomi the fool, the truth is, I was the fool. I knew that he had feelings for me but whatever he felt for me was not enough and would probably never be enough. Wes did not want all of me he only wanted a small part of me, and that hurt me more than I could bear. The knowledge of what I was to Wes encased my heart like a hard shell, leaving me hard, cold and bitter.

Gina and Melvin's love for each other grew unbridled and they both had changed as a result of it. Gina no longer sought the attention of men, the way she dressed was still sexy but more refined. Melvin obtained custody of his son Isaiah. The mother of Melvin's little boy was a crackhead who gave up her paternal rights for a steady supply of crack. Gina really came into her own as Isaiah's stepmother, she loved and cared for him better than his biological mother ever had. Although Gina and I did not party like we used to, we were still close. Gina and Melvin bought a house a few blocks from me and Gina and I were always in each other's homes. My friend was in love and Melvin loved her.

Gina and I were on our usual Saturday morning walk in the neighborhood trying to get our exercise in. We were not halfway through our walk when Gina stopped walking and bent over with her hands on her knees.

"Hey, slow down. I'm tired, girl," said Gina as she was panting trying to catch her breath.

"What's wrong with you?"

"Well, if you really want to know," said Gina as she straightened up and looked at me with a big old smile on her face.

"Yeah, I really want to know," I said as I stopped walking and turned around to look at her.

"I'm pregnant!"

I started screaming and walked back to Gina, hugged her and began rocking her from side to side.

"When are you due?"

"Next year in February."

"Gina, I'm so happy for you. Wow! A baby."

"Yeah, girl, and Melvin wants to get married after Christmas."

"That's only three months away!"

"I know, but it's going to be a small wedding, 50 people at the most. Eloise, I'm going to need your help planning my wedding, and Eloise will you be my maid of honor?"

"Of course, I will."

Gina and I decided to head back to her house. Melvin and Isaiah were sitting on the couch watching cartoons when Gina and I walked into the house.

"Good morning, fellas," I said as I walked in front of the TV on my way to the kitchen. I sat at the kitchen table while Gina got us both a glass of orange juice.

"What are you looking for?" I asked as I watched her open and close drawers.

"A pen and pad," she said as she finally found what she was looking for.

We spent most of the morning making a list of the things we needed to do and who was going to do it. When we got around to making the guest list, Gina was saying the names of the people to put on the guest list. When Wes and Naomi's names flowed out of her mouth it felt like Gina had hit me in my stomach. I tried to keep my face straight, but as I was sitting there thinking about it, I told Gina I could not be her maid of honor because

Naomi would know that Wes and I were messing around. Gina got really quiet and reached for my hand, holding it in hers.

"You're right. What are we going to do?" she asked so quietly that I almost didn't hear her.

"Gurl, don't worry about me. It's your wedding, and I can still help plan it."

"No, no . . . Eloise, you're my girl, you're going to be in my wedding," shouted Gina.

Melvin jumped up, came into the kitchen and asked what was going on.

"Eloise said she can't be in the wedding because Naomi would know they were back together if she knew me and Eloise are friends."

"Ah, shit, I didn't think about that," said Melvin as he looked in my direction, shook his head and looked down at the ground. Melvin turned around and left the room, leaving it to us to figure it out.

Gina said she would figure it out later. I agreed and left to go home. As I was walking back home, I felt an emptiness so complete I wondered how I was still alive. Each step toward my house was bringing me closer and closer to a world that only had room enough to contain me. I had never felt so alone. Because of the choices I made, I would never be a bride or a pregnant woman excitedly expecting a child. I had made Wes my whole world. I barely had enough energy to make it home. When I opened the front door to my house it no longer felt like a home, instead it felt like a movie set, where nothing was real. I told myself that this was our home, but Wes already had a home with his real family.

Gina and I continued to plan for her wedding. On the weekends we would go downtown and look at fabric, flowers, wedding favors, etc. Thanksgiving came around and I went to my parents as usual. I put on my happy face and lied to my parents about why Wes could not join us for Thanksgiving. Christmas came and went, and Gina's wedding day was almost here. Gina and I decided that I would wait until everyone was seated and I would look in the window of the foyer door of the church but would not go inside the sanctuary. Afterward I would go into the pastor's office where I would sign her marriage certificate as one of the witnesses.

The day of Gina and Melvin's wedding was cold but beautiful. The sky was baby blue with fluffy white clouds. I was at Gina's house with her mother and sisters. The music was playing, and the champagne was flowing. Gina was drinking water or juice, while we all catered to her. Finally, it was time to go to the church. Gina and her family got into the limousine and I followed in my car. When we got close to the church, I parked a couple of blocks from the church. I walked closer to the church as the late stragglers entered the church. I walked into the church's foyer after I heard the music that signaled Gina and her Father would be walking down the aisle. I walked into the church foyer just as the double door closed. I waited a little before I peeked into the window.

Gina and her father were more than halfway down the aisle. Melvin was sweating and smiling. Wes was standing beside his friend looking like a groom in his tux. Once Gina's father handed her over to the groom, everyone's back was to me, so I scanned the room looking for Naomi. I believe I spotted her, but I could not be sure. After Melvin kissed his bride I went to the pastor's office. I had to wait for the pictures to be taken so I looked around the office. Behind his desk was a bookshelf crammed with books and one entire shelf consisting of a variety of wooden and glass crosses.

While sitting in the pastor's office a quiet peace enveloped the room. A Bible was laying open on the desk. I picked up the Bible, which was opened to 1 Corinthians 13. My eyes fell on verse 4, I read verses 4 through part of verse 8 before Gina, Melvin, Wes and the Pastor walked in. The words of the scriptures were still twirling around in my head as I hugged Gina and Melvin. The Pastor had all of us sign the marriage certificate in the appropriate places. Gina and I hugged again before she and Melvin left the room. Wes gave me a peck on the check before he left, and the Pastor asked if I was OK. I told him I was fine, but I needed to wait for the wedding party to leave before I could leave. The Pastor sat in the chair behind his desk and I took a seat in one of the chairs in front of his desk.

"Why weren't you at the wedding?" asked the Pastor.

"I didn't want to be a distraction. I was trying to be charitable."

"I see," said the Pastor.

We sat in silence for a little while and I was just about to leave when the Pastor declared that God was gracious and loving, and that redemption was available to whosoever believed in his son, Jesus Christ. I told the Pastor that I was a Christian, that I believed in Jesus Christ, but it had been a long time since I was in church. He asked if I would like to rededicate my life to Christ.

"I'm not ready yet, Pastor, but I'll think about it. I think the coast is clear now. Thank you," I said as I got up to leave.

"Anytime young lady…remember our doors are always open."

I walked back into the foyer. I opened the door to the sanctuary and sat down in one of the pews. I rested my head on the pew in front of me and began to pray. I asked God to forgive me and I asked God to take him out of my life if I could not have him as my husband. I knew as I was praying that it would not be answered because it went against the will of God, but I prayed it anyway. I looked at the altar where Gina and Melvin took their vows, and I knew that I would never stand in front of a church and marry the man I loved; my father would never walk me down the aisle and give me away; my parents would never get to spoil any grandchildren if I stayed with Wes. I had wasted so much time trying desperately to have something that was not mine to have. Once again, I felt like dirt that you swept under the carpet and hoped no one noticed. Gina was the one who had been sleeping with two men. Gina was the one who had been taking money in exchange for sex. Yet she was the one that was saved from the wages of her sins, while I was left here all alone stuck in the muck and mire of my sins.

That night while Gina and Melvin were celebrating their marriage, I was home alone, a dirty little secret that would spoil the day if I, was, allowed to enter the room. That night I looked at Facebook and looked at all the postings of Gina and Melvin's wedding. There was a picture of Wes, Naomi, Gina and Melvin smiling at the camera. I felt so betrayed by Wes, Gina and Melvin. Gina was my friend, and I should have been the one in that picture. I should have been celebrating my friend's marriage. Tears rolled down my face, and the place where my heart was, began to hurt, and I remembered the scripture I read earlier in the pastor's office, 1 Corinthians 13: 4–8: "Charity suffereth long, and is kind; charity envieth not; charity vaunteth not itself, is not puffed up, 5: Doth not behave itself unseemly, seeketh not her own, is not easily provoked, thinketh no evil; 6: Rejoiceth not in iniquity, but rejoiceth in the truth; 7: Beareth all things, believeth all things, hopeth all things, endureth all things. 8: Charity never faileth . . ."

I cried myself to sleep that night thinking love had failed me. Because of my decision to lose my virginity that night, and a chance encounter with Wes, I had been walking around lost in the wilderness holding onto the very thing that was robbing me of a future where I did not have to hide, lie or pretend. I realized that night that I would never reach the promised land of milk and honey if I continued my relationship with Wes. I stood at a crossroad that night and made a decision that affected the rest of my life.

Chapter 8

Idid not see Gina again until it was close to her delivery date. I wanted to give Melvin and Gina their space. I had cooked dinner one Saturday and invited Gina, Melvin and Wes over. After dinner we were still seated at the dining room table, Wes was laughing at Melvin because he had put in an application down at the courtroom as a mail clerk. Melvin and Gina were growing apart from us, Wes did not know it, but I did. What they had found in each other was growing deep in the earth, establishing a foundation that would withstand the storms that were sure to come. Melvin gave up selling drugs because now he had something he could not afford to lose. I wished Melvin good luck and told him that I was sure he would get the job. Wes and Melvin went into the den to watch the game and Gina and I sat around the dining table, talking about work and how she could not wait for her last day at work before the baby came. I told Gina that she better come to work on her last day. Gina laughed and wanted to know why she needed to come to work on her last day.

"Don't worry about. I just need you to come to work on your last day."

"OK, girl," said Gina.

Melvin walked into the room and said they needed to get Isaiah from his mother's house. Gina and I hugged and said our goodbyes and I hugged Melvin goodbye. After they left, I asked Wes if he was staying the night, and he said that he was. Wes went back into the den to finish watching the game and I started to clean up the dining room and kitchen. After I finished cleaning up, I went into the den and sat next to Wes. I laid my head on his shoulder and began caressing him.

That night in bed, I watched Wes as he slept. I rolled over on my back and looked up at the ceiling. I wished that we could continue just as we were, but that would be at my detriment not his. Everyone was moving forward in their lives, while I was stuck in this place with Wes.

"I wished you had met me first." I whispered to the universe, thinking Wes was asleep.

"Huh…" said Wes, more asleep than awake.

"Nothing baby, go back to sleep."

That morning I got up before Wes did and had my coffee on the back porch. It was cold outside, but I found it peaceful watching the squirrel scurrying around in the yard and trees. I had to walk away before I lost myself and everything that made life worth living. I wanted what Gina and Melvin had, and I knew I could not have that with Wes. I was leaning on the rail with my coffee cup in my hand. I heard the kitchen door open and close, but I did not turn around. Wes leaned over me and hugged me.

"What's wrong, baby?"

"I did it for as long as I could, but I can't do any more."

"Did what?"

"Be with you."

"You got another man?"

"If I did…this would be easy."

We both stood there in silence, I with my back to him, Wes squeezed me tighter and buried his face into the folds of my robe, breathed in deeply and let his out breath loudly in my ear.

"Eloise, I'm giving you as much time as I can. I can try to get over here more often but that's going to be tough."

I struggled to turn around to look at him while he still held me in his arms. We looked at each for a long time. When I tried to pull out of this bear hug, he held on to me tighter, after I stopped struggling to be released, Wes opened my robe and looked at my nakedness. I do not know if he was deciding whether to leave his family or not.

"I need you," panted Wes.

"And I need you too," I said. "But not like this. Naomi is the mother of your first born child, your first wife…even if you left her for me…I know you're not going to, but…even if you left her for me, I would never be your first anything."

"What?" asked Wes, closing my robe and carefully tying it.

"All the things I am looking forward to, marriage and kids, you already have. It would never be as special to you as it would be for me. I would even give that up…I would give up being special if I could be your everything. I want a baby now, but I can't…not now, not like this."

Wes and I stood on the back porch leaning against each other, unable to find the words that would allow us to continue as we had.

"You're right. You are a good girl, Eloise. You deserve someone to love you like you want to be loved."

Wes looked down on me and sighed, after a while he opened the door and ushered me in.

"I'm going to take a shower, and then I'll leave." Wes said.

I was sitting at the dining room table when Wes came out the bedroom. He came into the dining room and sat across from me.

"You know I love you, but you're right. If you came first, you would have been the one. You are the one Eloise, but I got two kids, man."

"And a wife."

"And a wife," he chuckled, shook his head and got up from the chair, and then sat down again. The smile left his face when he told me that he loved me. Wes got up again and pulled his key chain out of his pocket.

It took him a few seconds to detach my key, but once he had done so he placed it on the table in front of me. I heard him open and close the front door, I sat there a long time after he pulled his car out of the driveway.

Chapter 9

On Gina's last day at work, I threw her a baby shower in my courtroom at lunch time. Gina was not surprised but she was touched that I would do that for her. She kept telling me that I should not have. Throwing a baby shower did not make up for not being in the room at her wedding; that hurt was still fresh. There was not enough time to open the presents, so we opened them up at Gina's house the next day, which was Saturday. Melvin and Isaiah were there when Gina opened her presents. Gina and I made running commentary on each gift. I made a list of who gave her what for the thank you cards. After all the gifts were opened, Gina and I started washing the baby clothes so we could put them up in the baby's room. Melvin took Isaiah to visit his grandmother.

Gina was sitting on the couch in the living room waiting for a load to finish so we could start another load.

"Have you heard from Wes?" asked Gina.

"He called once wanting to know if I was okay. Wes was never going to leave his kids, and the truth be told he wasn't going to leave Naomi."

"Are you OK?"

"Nope, but I'm going to be. All I know is that if I didn't let Wes go, then another five, ten years would go by, and nothing would have changed. Besides gurl, I want what you got. I want to have a baby, and I guess a husband comes with that," I said laughing.

Gina reached over and tried to hug me, but she was having trouble trying to get to me.

"What you doing?" I asked, laughing and scooting over so she could reach me. We sat there laughing in each other's arms.

"It's hard, being without him. I want him back so bad, but I can't anymore. We had some good times, the four of us, but when Melvin stepped up and made you his woman, then quit the game and got a 9 to 5, that's when I knew Wes would never give up his family for me."

"You're going to find someone, you will. Give yourself some time to get over him. When I drop this baby, give me a few months and I'll be your wing man," said Gina as she leaned back laughing and holding her stomach.

I missed Gina not being at work. Even though we did not see each other every day, we tried to have lunch when we could, but I knew she was there if I needed her. Once again, I was alone. I did not have my girl Gina to kick it with, and I did not have Wes. I stopped looking at Naomi's Facebook page, but I could not stop feeling like Wes was still here with me. Every room in my house was filled with the memory of us. The den was the room we loved watching TV in, either lying on the floor or cuddled on the couch, the backyard is where we hung out in the summer having impromptu barbecues, laughing and drinking around the fire pit.

Sometimes in the middle of the night I would sit up in bed, heart pounding, sensing something was wrong; after a few seconds, I would remember what was wrong. My heart would slow down, and a sadness would settle on me because Wes was not coming back. Sometimes I would lay back down and imagine Wes lying next to me with his arms around me. Sometimes I would lay there in the dark and wonder if Wes was making love to Naomi, or if he was lying in the dark thinking of me.

Gina was a week past her due date when she finally went into labor. Melvin called me about 11:00 p.m. and I jumped up and went over to their house to watch Isaiah. I parked in front of the house and ran to the front door, which opened before I could knock on it.

"Isaiah is asleep in his bed. I'll call you when the baby's here," said Melvin. Gina was hanging on to Melvin for dear life. Her eyes were bucked out and I could tell she was scared.

I hugged Gina and whispered in her ear, "You can do this." Gina squeezed me and told me she got this.

Melvin called me eight hours later to tell me that Gina and baby Melba were fine, and he would be home in a couple of hours.

After Melvin made it home, I went to my house, showered, changed and went to the hospital to see Gina and the baby. I was sitting in the waiting room when Wes showed up. He came over and said hello. I told him that there were too many people in the room, and I was waiting for someone to come out. As we were sitting there talking about Melvin, Gina and the baby I sneaked a close look at his face. I noticed creases by his eyes and lines around his mouth.

"How's everything with you?" I asked.

"It's all good," said Wes with a thin smile. "You're looking good. Wassup with you?"

"Nothing much. I'm just working and trying to stay busy."

"That's wassup."

Just then Gina's mother and sisters walked into the waiting area having come from Gina's room. Wes and I said hello, got up and hugged everybody, then walked down the hall to Gina's room. Gina was lying in bed holding her baby girl. Wes and I stayed in the room until Melvin came in. When Melvin saw his friend, he got emotional. They clasped hands like black men do. While their hands were still clasped Melvin pulled Wes to him and hugged his brother. All of us in the same room felt like old times. Our spirits were lifted, and we were all smiling happy to be in each other's presence. Melvin was introducing us to his daughter. Gina was telling us how much she weighed and how long she was. Melvin and Gina's joy were contagious. Wes and I looked into each other's eyes and smiled. Hating for this moment to pass, but also knowing that we could not stay in it forever, Wes and I said our goodbyes. Wes took my hand in his as we walked down the hall. We said goodbye to Gina's family so they could go back in the room and continued to walk hand in hand to the front of the hospital. We stopped when we got outside the hospital. Wes leaned down and brushed his lips across my lips. I reached up and hugged the man I loved with all my heart. I stepped back and looked deeply into his eyes.

"Take care of yourself, Wes. Be careful in them streets."

"I will and you too, baby girl".

I turned and began to walk away from the man I had given so much of myself to. I gave to him my body and he gave me his. He taught my body how to respond to his touch exclusively. I gave him my heart, so soft and tender, a heart that like my body responded to his voice, his touch, his presence. I pinned my hope in him and hung in there longer than I should have. I compromised my integrity, trying to hang on to a love that was not destined to be but refused to die. I knew I would love Wes for the rest of my life whether I ever saw him again or not. I also knew that Wes loved me. I turned around hoping to catch one last glimpse of him. He was standing there directly under a streetlight and there was a glow around him. I could not see his features, but I knew he was smiling, because I was smiling. I turned back around and crossed the street. The sadness that I wore like a garment for so long that I could not remember when I put it on, slipped off my shoulders and down my back. That hollow feeling in my heart was still there but not as pronounced. Loving Wes would always be bittersweet. A sweet encounter that was only meant to last one night, but the unexpected happened and love took root and grew where it was not supposed to. That love which was so sweet in the beginning almost left me broken and bitter. As I got into my car and drove out of the parking lot, I turned left hoping Wes would still be where I saw him last. I just wanted to see his smile one more time. When I got to the spot where he was earlier, there was no one there.

Chapter 10

The house I bought to live out my fantasy began to close in on me. Everywhere I looked reminded me of him, of us. I remembered how Wes loved to get the yard ready for our backyard barbeques. Wes would mow the lawn, trim the hedges while I raked the leaves and replaced either dead or dying plants. The neighbors probably thought we were a married couple who liked to entertain. Those days were almost perfect; almost because, the fairytale ended when Wes had to go back to his real home, back to his real family.

I was sitting in the backyard looking at the hedges that needed trimming and the flower bed that needed weeding thinking maybe it would be easier if I sold this house and started fresh so I would not be reminded daily of him. Other days I would wander around the house with a smile on my face thinking about how we would spend the day lying around either in bed on the couch or on the floor in the den watching TV. Finally, I got up from the chair I was sitting in and went to the shed to get the hedge clippers. I was so focused on the hedges that I did not hear Gina open the side gate when she stepped into the backyard with baby Melba and said hello, she startled me. I turned around and smiled immediately when I saw Gina and the baby. I sat the clippers down on the ground and grabbed Melba out of her mother's arms.

"I've been banging on the front door, then it dawned on me that you were probably in the backyard. How have you been doing?" asked Gina.

"I'm good, girl. How have you been doing?" I asked as I hugged her with one arm while I held Melba in my other.

Gina and I sat down on the rattan couch and Melba started crying for her mommy. I leaned over and handed her back to her mother.

"I made some lemonade would you like a glass?"

"Yeah, that sounds good."

When I got back with Gina's lemonade, Melba was asleep in her mother's arms.

"She's so beautiful, Gina!"

"Thanks," said Gina with a broad smile on her face.

"Look at all that hair and her fat legs!"

We both sighed and looked down at Melba. Gina looked at me and asked me not to get mad because she had to tell me something.

"Mad, why would I get mad at you?"

"Well," Gina said, clearing her throat as she sat up straight and looked me in the eyes. "You know Melvin and Wes are like brothers, so you know they still get together from time to time. So, you know Naomi and I have had to get together from time to time as well. You know that you're my girl and that's why I'm letting you know that Naomi and I get together sometimes."

Gina and I just looked at each other for a few uncomfortable minutes, and I willed myself not to cry. I could feel the tears gathering in my eyes, but I refused to let them fall.

I had to clear my throat before I could speak. "What do you mean you and Naomi get together from time to time?"

"Well, you know she has come over to the house to see the baby, and sometimes when we go to Melvin's mother's house we stop by Naomi and Wes's place."

"Oh."

"And, because Cassius and Isaiah are almost the same age they get together and play, so sometimes Naomi visits for a little bit when she drops off or picks up Cassius."

"Oh, so you guys are friends now?"

"Well, you know, we're not friends, but we are friendly."

"Does she know that we're friends?"

"No," said Gina, as she laid Melba across her lap, and then looked up at me.

"Gina, what do you want me to do or say? I can't tell you not to be her friend, but are you telling me that you can't be my friend?"

"No, no, no, I'm not saying that. I just wanted you to know that I'm getting to know Naomi and we get together from time to time."

"Okay, Gina, well thanks for letting me know. I understand. Girl, I would love to sit here and talk all day, but I got to get back to these hedges before it gets dark," I said as I stood up signaling the end to her visit.

I got up picked up the clippers and began trimming the hedges. Gina said OK and something else I did not hear as she left the same way she came. After she left, I sat back on the couch and that is when the tears fell from my eyes. I just lost my best friend. I sat in the backyard until it was getting dark, and the mosquitoes started munching on my ankles. Well, I thought to myself as I walked in the back door; there is nothing left for me here. I could sell the house and buy something else somewhere else. Weeks went by and I did not hear from Gina. She did not call, and I did not call her. I was not angry at her, but I was hurt. She was in an awkward position, I knew that, but she was my friend, and yet Naomi had won again.

One day at work, several months after she left my backyard, I saw Gina walking down the hallway. She and I were walking toward each other. When we met, we hugged and said hello. I asked how everyone was doing and she asked how my parents were doing. Gina told me that Melba was walking now, and that is when it hit me that I was no longer in her life anymore, I was relegated to acquaintance status, because friends shared their lives with each other, and I was missing out on the milestones of Gina's life. I did a quick calculation in my head and realized that Melba had to be one-year-old, and I am sure Gina threw a birthday party for her. I could have left it there, just a supposition in my head, but I wanted Gina to confirm my suspicion.

"How old is Melba now?"

"She's 14 months," said Gina smiling.

"Did you have a birthday party for her?" I asked trying to keep my voice light and carefree.

"Well, you know, we just had a small little something for her at the house, just family and a few...other people," said Gina her smile sliding off her face as she realized that I was no longer considered her friend.

"Were Wes and Naomi there?" I asked not bothering to keep my voice light or carefree, because I cared, and Gina knew I cared about the answer to this question.

"Yeah, they were. They brought the boys. Girl, I got to get back to my courtroom and try and catch up on my backlog," Gina said already walking away from me.

Okay, I thought as I watched Gina walk away. Does Gina need to hit you over the head with a two by four for you to know she is no longer your friend?

That night when I went home, I decided that I would rent my house out and move into a small apartment until I was ready to move back into my home. That weekend I started looking for apartments. Apartments in Pasadena were too expensive if I was going to save money, so I started looking in the Crenshaw area. I started boxing up my possessions that I would take with me and getting rid of the things I no longer needed. I hired a realtor to lease out my house, and she also helped me find an apartment to live in. The apartment was a Spanish style building in Leimert Park. The street was lined with apartment buildings with an occasional single-family house. The area was nice, and I felt safe. It was hard leaving my house, but I knew it was the right thing for me to do if I wanted to heal.

Chapter 11

I loved my new place. The complex consisted of four individual one-bedroom one-bath units with their own courtyard. My unit had hardwood floors in the living room, hallway and bedroom and terracotta tiles in the bathroom and kitchen. I brought my old furniture that fit in my new place with me and put the rest in storage. My beloved Ficus tree was doing well in its new location, so the place immediately felt like home without all the baggage. Apparently, vacancies did not come up that frequently here, so all the neighbors knew each other and were very protective of their slice of paradise. Every Friday the neighbors got together at each other's homes and had wine and hors d'oeuvres at whoever was hosting, and if we were in the mood a spontaneous potluck would occur. On those occasions we would listen to music and play cards until the host kicked us out. Our cast of characters consisted of Ms. Mildred, who was elderly and lived alone but her grandson Nate checked on her; Valerie, who was in her mid-thirties and her unemployed husband, Charlie, who she supported; Ms. Mabel, who was also elderly but had no one to check up on her, so we all checked on her, and finally me. To say I loved living there would be an understatement. God knew exactly what I needed when he placed me there.

It was one of our usual Friday nights and I was hosting our wine and whine Friday. Valerie and I were in the kitchen sipping our wine and complaining about our work week and how glad we were that it was over. Valerie's husband, Charlie, usually did not attend the Friday night get together and tonight was no exception. Ms. Mildred and Ms. Mabel were on the couch munching on chips and salsa. The microwave timer dinged, and I got the taco bites out of the oven and placed them on the serving trays. Just then there was a knock on the door; Mildred and Mabel yelled for whoever was at the door to come in.

"Hey, baby," said Ms. Mildred when she saw her grandson walk through the door.

"Hi, Grandma. Hello, everyone," said Nate.

Valerie and I came from the kitchen each holding a tray of taco bites. I put my tray on the coffee table and looked up into Nate's eyes. Damn, that's a good-looking man was the first thought that sprung to my mind. I guessed that he was about 6'2, and had beautiful dark brown skin, black hair shaved close to his head, thick eyebrows, long lashes and dimples. Nate smiled down at me and I introduced myself. I offered him a glass of wine which he declined, but asked if I had any beer, when I told him I was sorry I did not, he excused himself and stated that he would be back. We were all sitting in the living room when Nate came back with a six-pack of beer. He pulled a can from the pack and asked if anyone wanted a beer. Ms. Mabel said she would take one for later. Nate wanted to know if he could put the rest in the refrigerator. I told him yes and got up to take the beer. I came back into the living room with a kitchen chair for Nate and told him to help himself to chips, salsa and taco bites. Nate got a plate off the coffee table and filled it with taco bites, chips and salsa and sat next to me. We talked about current events, politics and whatever else was trending on the news. Nate told us he was off for a couple of days but would be driving a load to New York next week. As we were eating talking and drinking, Nate's knee would occasionally brush my thigh sparking a tingling sensation from my thigh that ended in the pit of my stomach. I could not tell if he was intentionally touching me and I wondered if he was feeling what I was feeling.

Valerie was the first to leave, because she had to fix Charlie's dinner. Ten minutes later Ms. Mabel got up to leave; Ms. Mildred and Nate said they were leaving as well.

"Thank you, guys, for coming. As usual I had a good time. Nate, don't forget your beer."

"Oh, no that's for you," said Nate.

"No, you take them, I don't drink beer." I replied.

"Naw, you keep them that way you'll have a beer for me when I come back. Do you mind if I come back sometime?"

"No, I don't mind." I said feeling shy and silly all at the same time.

Nate helped his grandmother up from the couch and stood looking at me with a smile on his face as he opened the door for her and Ms. Mabel.

After everyone had gone, I was picking up the dishes and putting the chairs back in the kitchen when I realized I was smiling and that my jaws hurt from smiling.

Nate started dropping by my place when he came to check on his grandmother. One Friday he made chili and I made the cornbread for his grandmother's potluck. Nate was a long-haul trucker and was gone for long periods of time so I did not spend as much time with him as I would have liked. One Saturday I was helping Ms. Mildred weed her garden when Nate walked into her courtyard.

"Hey, Grandma," said Nate as he walked over to his grandmother and kissed her on the cheek.

"Hi, baby," said Ms. Mildred.

"How you doing, Eloise?"

"I'm good. How are you?"

"I'm all right. Just a little tired. Grandma, what you got to eat?"

"I'm going to cook some of these greens when we finish up here."

"Eloise, what you cooking today?" asked Nate as he stood grinning down at me.

"I don't know. What you want me to cook?" I asked looking up, grinning back at him.

"So, you're going to cook me anything I want?"

"No that's not what I meant. I'll cook you whatever you want if I have the ingredients. So, what do you want?"

"What you got?"

"I don't know, boy, I have to look."

"Well, when you're done let me know and I'll walk over and see what you got."

Nate walked into the side door of Ms. Mildred's unit. As I finished weeding, dead heading and picking collard greens, Nate was cleaning Ms. Mildred's unit.

I heard the vacuum cleaner, and watched Nate take the trash out to the big trash bin in the back of the complex. When he came back, he told his grandmother he was done cleaning the house and wanted to know if there was anything else, she needed done. She told him no and thanked him for his help. Finally, I finished with Ms. Mildred's garden, Nate and I said goodbye to Ms. Mildred as she wobbled into her apartment.

As soon as I unlocked my door and stepped inside my apartment, Nate went immediately to the refrigerator and looked inside.

"Man, you don't have anything in here!" Nate exclaimed.

"OK, we can go to the store and get something to cook."

"I'm hungry now! Do you like Japanese food?" he asked while he was still looking in the refrigerator.

"Yeah, I know a new place. It's on Crenshaw just before you get to the freeway."

"Yeah, I know it. It's good. So, what do you want?"

"I always get the tuna bowl."

"Anything else?"

"No, that's plenty. Do you want me to come with you or can I stay and take a bath?"

He came out of the kitchen and stood close to me sniffing the air.

"Yeah, you can stay," he said laughing. "I'll be right back."

While Nate was getting the food, I turned on the radio, changed the sheets on my bed and took a quick shower.

I was sitting on the couch with the front door open looking out the screen door. I was asking myself if I was ready to start something with Nate. I knew we had been leading up to this for a while now. When Nate was in town, we would kick it together. Sometimes we would catch a movie or grab something to eat, with or without Ms. Mildred. So, I knew when Nate came back that we would probably end up in bed. Nate was a good-looking man with a J.O.B. That alone should have been enough to bed him down, but what was so compelling to me was that he was good to his grandmother, and I liked that. I was still sitting there lost in thought when Nate opened the screen door holding two big bags.

"Wow! What did you get?"

"I got me some beer, and you some wine."

"Good, let's eat!"

After we ate Nate said he was really tired. He said he could either go to his grandmother's place and take a nap or he could take a nap here if I did not mind. I told him I did not mind and walked him to my bedroom. I was just turning to go back to the living room when Nate asked me to lay down with him. I walked around the bed and laid on top of the covers next to him. Nate pulled me to him and laid an arm on my stomach. I lay there waiting for him to make his move, when I realized that his heavy breathing was not because I was lying next to him but because he was asleep. After I was sure he was sound asleep I got up and went back into the living room.

I was sitting on the couch watching TV, when Nate walked into the living room.

"You must have been tired. You've been asleep for a minute."

"Yeah, I was but I'm good now." Nate went to the kitchen and got a beer out of the refrigerator and yelled from the kitchen, "Do you want a glass of wine?"

"Yeah, I'll take a glass."

Nate came back into the living room with a can of beer and my wine in a water glass.

"What is this?" I laughed.

"Your wine," said Nate very slowly, as if he was speaking to someone who had difficulty understanding things.

"Who drinks wine in a water glass?" I asked in a snooty voice. I got up from the couch and took the glass from his hand and went back to the kitchen and poured my wine into a wine glass, after which I went back into the living room and sat next to Nate on the couch. He was drinking his beer and I began to sip my wine.

"Are you hungry?" I asked.

"Yep."

"There's plenty of food left. Do you want me to fix you a plate?"

"I don't want no food," said Nate looking at me intensely.

"But you said you were hungry. Oh! . . ."

"I am hungry, Eloise. What about you? You hungry?"

"Um hum."

Nate put his beer on the coffee table and took my wine glass out of my hands and put it on the coffee table as well. Then he kissed me and leaned me back on the couch, my body responded, and I remembered everything Wes taught me. Nate was gentle and kind as we made love on the couch.

That night as we were lying in bed, I told Nate I was still in love with someone else, but that I was trying to move on. Nate just looked at me as I told him about Wes. After I finished, he sighed and told me how he was in love with someone who he had lost to drugs and how she was now out on the streets selling her body. He told me they lived together almost 3 years and that she cheated on him and broke his heart, but he took her back and she cheated on him again. By that time, he knew she had a drug habit, so he started taking her on runs with him and buying her drugs so she would not have to sell herself for drugs until he could not look himself in the mirror. Nate told me how on their last haul together they were at a truck stop and she wanted some crack, he told her he was not going to buy her anymore drugs, but he would get her some help when they got back home.

"She started crying, and told me how she wanted help, but could I get her one last hit before we got back home. I told her I would, so I got out of the truck to get us some food and to see if I could find somebody selling crack. I had the food and was walking toward my truck while looking down the lines of parked rigs to see if anyone was doing drugs or selling drugs when I saw her stop a trucker as he was pulling off. She looked back at my truck as she was getting into his truck. She didn't see me, but I saw her, and I saw the smile she had on her face as she climbed into the cab of his truck." Nate stopped talking and looked up at the ceiling for a minute or two; he cleared his throat and continued telling me about the woman that broke his heart.

"I didn't see Malissa again for about eight months after that. She was at one of the truck- stops I usually stopped at; she was skin and bones. I brought her some food and tried to talk her into coming back with me so I could get her some help, or take her to her momma's house, anywhere she wanted to go, anywhere, but I couldn't get her to come with me. I started stopping at truck-stops hoping to see her. When I was lucky enough to see her, I would buy her food, and ask her if she was ready to come home," said Nate exhaling at the end of the story, exhausted from the telling.

After Nate finished his story, we lay in each other's arms thinking our own thoughts. I do not know what made me tell Nate that I was still in love with Wes. I guessed I just wanted to be honest, and he seemed relieved after having told me about Malissa. I went to sleep in his arms that night, and the next morning I woke up first, and lay there looking at him, I was thinking how one never knew what people were going through. I would have never guessed that Nate was so broken, his scars could not be seen by the naked eye; his façade was smooth and quiet; his wounds lay deep beneath his beautiful dark skin. I looked at him wondering if I could be the one to save him from his loneliness and maybe while I was saving him, he could save me. Nate touched me in a place where only one other person had touched me before. As those thoughts drifted through my mind Nate opened his eyes, and we looked at each other for a long while before we touched each other again.

Chapter 12

Nate was a truck driver who drove a big rig for a trucking company. Most of his jobs were long hauls to the east coast, but on occasions he did short hauls to Las Vegas. I went with him sometimes on short hauls to Vegas. One time we were on our way back from Vegas when Nate pulled off the 15 Freeway in Victorville, California. We drove up Bear Valley Road and Nate showed me a community called Spring Valley. I could not believe how beautiful it was. I did not know much about Victorville, but what I had heard about it was negative, so I was pleasantly surprised. The homes were not the typical track homes; each house was different, and the area had mature trees. Quite a few of the homes had grass lawns instead of desert landscaping. Because the area was elevated, some of the homes had awesome views of the valley below. The thing that really blew my mind was the marina. There were homes that backed up to a manmade lake and had their own docks. After Nate showed me the area, we got back on the freeway to go home. Nate dropped me off at my place; he used the bathroom and got back in his truck so that he could drop his load. I checked in on Ms. Mildred and let her know that we made it back and Nate would be back soon.

"Y'all come back for dinner. I'm frying some chicken; I can do mashed potatoes, gravy and greens. What you think, does that sound good?"

"That sounds good! I'll call him and let him know that you're cooking." I gave Ms. Mildred a peck on the cheek and told her I would be back in a little bit.

I called Nate and let him know that his grandmother was cooking, then I watered my plants. I made myself a cup of tea and sat down on the couch enjoying my tea and a little time to myself. As I was sitting on the couch looking out of the window, I suddenly became overwhelmed as I realized how blessed I was. Nate and I were falling in love, I had a good job, I had my health, and my parents were good. I sat there watching the dappled sunlight dance on the hardwood floor. When the wind blew the leaves on the tree outside my window, the sunlight created different patterns on the floor. I felt so peaceful watching the changing patterns and sipping my tea. When I finished my tea, I got up and went to help Ms. Mildred with dinner.

Chapter 13

For the first time in a long time, I was happy. I knew Nate still loved Malissa, and I still loved Wes, but what we felt for each other was not overshadowed by what we felt for Malissa and Wes. I no longer looked at Naomi's Facebook page. Well, I did not look at it as often as I used to. It was going to be my birthday in a couple of weeks, and I wanted to do something special with Nate. Nate assured me that he would be back in time for my birthday, and he wanted me to be packed and ready to go when he got there.

On my birthday, I was like a kid, dressed and waiting for Nate to arrive. I was standing in the doorway looking out the screen door watching Nate walk up the courtyard walkway. Nate waved and said he would be back after he checked on his Grandma. I sighed, left the doorway and went to the bathroom. After checking to make sure I had everything, I checked my makeup, applied more lipstick and fluffed my twist. Nate was walking down the walkway toward my unit as I was locking the front door. Nate kissed me on the lips and took my overnight bag as we walked to his car.

"Where are we going?" I asked the minute we got in the car.

"You'll see."

I was not surprised when he turned east on the 10 Freeway, and I was not surprised when we turned onto the 15 Freeway going north, but I was surprised when we exited onto Bear Valley Road. What the hell, I was thinking to myself. I looked over at Nate and all I saw from the side of his face was his dimpled cheek.

"Where are we going?" I asked, but this time not so sweetly.

"You'll see."

I was pissed, so I just folded my arms, sighed and tried to keep my mouth closed.

The neighborhood we were driving in was beautiful, and he stopped in front of a single-story house with a big tree in the yard, with a curved walkway flanked by a nice green lawn. The house was a traditional ranch with brick at the bottom and batten board at the top. Nate got out of the car, but I remained in the car. Nate walked around the front of the car, over to my side and opened my door. I got out, willing myself to keep my mouth clamped. He took my hand and we walked up to the front door. Nate knocked on the door, no answer.

We walked back to the car, but before we got back in the car Nate stopped and looked at the house.

"Nice house, huh?"

"Yeah, it's really nice. Who lives here?"

Nate dug his hand in his pocket and pulled out a key and placed it in my hand.

"We do."

"What? We do?"

Nate pulled me by my hand and walked me back to the front door.

"Open the door, babe."

My hand was trembling as I put the key in the lock. I opened the door. The door opened into the living room and dining area on one side and on the other side was another room with a large opening instead of a door. Past the dining area was the kitchen which opened to a large family room. The family room had a fireplace and sliding glass doors that opened to the backyard. The backyard had a paved enclosed patio, several trees and a lawn. I backtracked to the front and turned left down the hallway to look at three bedrooms and a hall bathroom. At the end of the hallway was the large master bedroom which had a sliding glass door leading to the backyard. The master bathroom had double sinks, a free-standing tub and a shower and a water closet.

As I was walking from room to room, Nate was walking behind me not saying a word.

"How big is this thing?"

"2500 square feet. Do you like it?"

"No, I love it!"

"Don't you remember this house?"

"No, I just remember the area was so nice and I loved all the houses. This is beautiful Nate, I'm so happy for you!"

Nate put his arms around me and asked if I was happy for us.

"What do you mean 'us'?"

"Eloise . . . will you marry me?"

"Yes, yes I will." I answered without hesitation.

We kissed and stood hugging each other. I was hugging the man that just proposed to me, but I was thinking about the man I was still in love with. I finally got to hear those words, "Will you marry me?" but they were not coming from the man I waited for what felt like my entire life to say, but they were coming from a good man, one I knew I could build a life with.

The day that Nate proposed to me was a happy one, and I knew that Nate could make me happy, and I believed that I could make him happy. That night as Nate and I slept on an air mattress, I lay there thinking about Wes. I silently wiped away tears. I could put my life on hold waiting for something that was never going to happen, or I could take a leap of faith and try to be happy with Nate. I did not want to hurt Nate, but Nate would always be my second choice, and I knew that was not fair to him, but life was not fair, I knew I would never have who I really wanted, so I decided that I would marry Nate and be a good wife to him, vowing that he would never know that he was my second choice. The next day Nate and I drove to Vegas to tell my parents that we were engaged. Mom was watering her flowers when we pulled up in front of her house. She did a second take when she realized it was me getting out of the car.

"Hey, baby!" squealed Mom as she flapped both her arms, even though she was holding the water hose in her right hand. Mom's arms stopped flapping when she saw Nate getting out of the car. I hugged Mom before she could turn off the water. Nate was standing behind me when Mom and I finished hugging. I turned around and introduced Nate to my mother.

"Nate this is my mother, Elizabeth Wallace."

"Nice to meet you, Mrs. Wallace." Nate said as he extended his hand.

She batted his hand away and gave him a hug.

"Call me Beth or Mom," said my mother when she released him.

"Y'all go in the house and say hello to your daddy. He's either in the family room or upstairs watching TV. I'm be in when I finish watering my roses."

Nate and I walked in the front door. Dad looked around when he heard the door open.

"Hey, baby!" said Dad as he struggled to get up from the couch. Dad and I hugged, and Nate and Dad shook hands as I introduced Nate to my Dad.

"Dad, this is Nate, and Nate this is my Dad, Arthur Wallace."

"Nice to meet you, Mr. Wallace."

"Nice to meet you, too, son. Y'all have a sit. You didn't tell us you were coming," declared my Dad as he took his seat again. Nate sat on the couch next to him and I sat in one of the side chairs.

"I didn't know I was coming either. We just decided this morning to come and see you guys," I stated.

"Me and your Mom called you yesterday for your birthday, but you didn't answer the phone."

"Sorry, Dad, my phone must be acting up," I said trying to keep a straight face; just then Mom came into the house.

"Baby, we tried to call you yesterday for your birthday, but you didn't answer the phone."

"Dad was telling me that. Sorry, Mom. I didn't know you called. My phone must be acting up."

"What y'all doing here on a weekday, did you take off work for your birthday?" asked Mom.

"Yeah, Mom, I took three days off."

"Y'all plan on staying here for a few days?" asked my Mom.

I looked at Nate before I answered, but before I could answer Nate did.

"We could, if you don't mind, I just wanted to come and meet you because I asked your daughter something yesterday. I been seeing your daughter for a few months, maybe eight, nine months. I know it's not a lot of time, but I love her, and she loves me. I probably should have asked you, sir, before I asked Eloise, but we wanted to know if we could have your blessings."

"Oh my God!" screamed my Mother, as my Dad sat there staring at Nate.

"Do you mean to tell me that you asked my daughter to marry you?" asked my Father.

"Yes, sir."

Nate and my Father were looking at each when my Mother grabbed me from my seat and hugged me. My Father looked at Nate and asked him how could, he give him his blessing when he did not know anything about him. Nate agreed and proceeded to tell my Dad and Mom all about him-self. He told them that he was a truck driver and had been driving trucks for over 10 years. He told them how it was just him and his grandmother that he checked on whenever he was in town. He also told them that he just bought a house in Victorville, and how he wanted to start a family immediately. When Nate was finished, we were all looking at my Father, who seem to be mulling over everything Nate had said. My Dad looked at me and asked me if I loved this man.

"Yeah, Daddy, I love him."

"Well, that's good enough for me. Y'all got my blessings," he said as he got up. Nate stood up and shook my Dad's hand. My Dad said he was tired and was going upstairs to lay down for a bit. My Mom got up from her chair and hugged Nate, welcoming him to the family. I watched Dad walk up the stairs. Mom was asking us when we thought we were going to get married and when were we going to start making babies. I told Nate and Mom I would be right back. Dad was lying down in bed watching TV when I came into his room.

"Dad, what's wrong?"

"Nothing baby, I'm just tired."

"Tell me the truth. If you don't want me to marry him, I won't, but I really want to be married when I start having kids." I said smiling trying to make him smile.

"You pregnant?"

"No, Dad, I'm not pregnant."

"What happened to that other fella, Wes?"

"It didn't work out."

"Does this Nate guy treat you good?"

"Yeah, Dad, Nate treats me good."

"You not just marrying him because he's the first guy to ask you? Are you?"

Damn. Dad hit the nail straight on the head, but I could not tell him that.

"No, I'm marrying him because I want to marry him, and he loves me. I think we can have a good life together just like you and Mom."

Dad smiled at that and reached for my hand.

"Okay, baby girl, I'm happy for you guys, and I'll be down in a little bit."

"Okay, Dad," I bent down and kissed his forehead before I walked out of the room.

For the next couple of days, Dad and Mom got to know Nate. We went to the casinos and played bingo and the slot machines with my parents. Nate took them out to breakfast one day and dinner the next day. He did everything he could to show them that he was going to be a good husband and son-in-law. By the time we left to go home Mom and Dad were calling him Son, and Nate was calling them Mom and Dad.

When we got back home Ms. Mildred was so happy because she already knew Nate's plans to ask me to marry him and she also knew about the house. Ms. Mildred, Nate and I celebrated that night at her place. Nate and I were getting ready to leave when Ms. Mildred told me to sit with her for a spell. Nate kissed his Grandma goodnight and left to go to my unit.

"You know I lost my daughter a long time ago. I raised Nate since he was a little boy. That boy has grown into a good man. When I lost my daughter to drugs, to the streets, that hurt, but when she overdosed it was a hurting pain that creeps up on me from time to time, even after all these years. If it hadn't been for that little boy, I don't know what I would have done. I don't think I would have made it through all that pain."

Ms. Mildred stopped talking as she tried to collect herself. Ms. Mildred reached out and held my hand in both of hers. I did not say anything, waiting for her to gain control of the emotions she was battling. Tears were glistening in her eyes and her face was contorted with pain.

"He's already had his heart broken. Did he tell you about that?" asked Ms. Mildred.

"Yes. He told me."

"That girl broke his heart, and that was hard to watch. I don't want to have to watch that again. I'm asking you not to break his heart. You're a good girl, Eloise, and I think you guys will be good for each other. Do you think you're ready to be married?"

"Yes, madam, I'm ready. I love your grandson, and I know he's a good man, because I see how he treats you. I have no intention of hurting him."

"Well, that's good to know, sweetheart. I want you to know I'm glad you're going to be my daughter. Now help me off this couch so I can go to bed."

I helped Ms. Mildred up, she walked me to the door and hugged me as she told me goodnight.

"Goodnight, Momma," I whispered in her ear.

"Goodnight, Daughter."

Chapter 14

Nate and I decided that we would fix up the house instead of having a big wedding. Nate left the renovations up to me since he was gone most of the time. Every time Nate was in town he would go to the house and see the progress of the renovations. Nate was walking around looking at everything, and I was pointing out that the only thing left to do was the carpeting which was being installed next Saturday.

"So, when do you want to move in?" asked Nate.

"Well, I gave my notice already, so next month. Once the carpets are installed, I can start bringing the small stuff. Between what I have in my place and what I have in storage we should be okay for now. We can take our time and get more stuff later. Will you be back in time for the move, or do we need to hire someone to help me move?"

"I'll be back around the 3rd, so see if the landlord will let you stay an extra week. I can get Charlie to help us load the stuff out of your unit and storage."

"Okay, I'll check with the landlord. It should be okay."

Nate continued to look at the bathroom where a new vanity, granite, mirrors and tile had been installed.

"You did a good job. Everything looks good," Nate said.

"I know, right! I can't wait to move in."

Nate locked the house before we headed back down the hill to my apartment.

Moving day finally arrived. I do not know who was more excited, me or Nate. Charlie and Valerie were a big help. Between the four of us we got the truck loaded and were on our way to the house before noon. Valerie rode with me, and we stopped and got a bucket of chicken and sides. I had already had water, sodas and beer in a cooler in the back of my car.

"This is nice, girl," said Valerie as I pulled up to the house.

"Thanks, I love it."

Nate and Charlie had started unloading the stuff. Boxes were in the front room, and Nate and Charles had put the couch in the family room. I put the food on the island in the kitchen and went back to the car for the drinks. Instead of trying to carry the cooler into the house, I just got a liter of soda, and a six-pack of beer. Charlie was getting boxes out of the truck when I told him to come on in and get something to eat. Nate and I ran into each other in the kitchen, and I told him to stop for a minute and eat. Valerie was busy giving herself a self-guided tour of the house when she finally came into the kitchen to make herself a plate. Charlie was sitting on the couch with his food, so Valerie took her place next to him with her plate. Nate and I were seated next to each other on the floor.

"Man, this is nice, man." Said Charlie.

"Thanks, man. Eloise did a great job with the place. You should have seen it before she put her touch on it." Explained Nate.

As we were eating and talking about the house, Charlie and Valerie were saying how they could never afford something this nice. Nate and I laughed and said we could not either, that is why we bought something out in Timbuktu. We were talking and laughing about how crazy my commute was going to be, when Nate got quiet and told Charlie that his company was always looking for drivers, and how he got started. Valerie looked over at Charlie smiling and Charlie looked at Valerie smiling and told Nate that he would definitely check that out.

It was dark by the time Nate came back from dropping off Charlie, Valerie and the moving truck. I was lying in bed exhausted when I heard him come into the house.

"It's me, babe," yelled Nate from the front room.

Nate lay across the bed saying he was too tired to take his clothes off let alone take a shower.

"I know, but I put clean sheets on this bed, so you better get up and take a shower before you get under these covers," I said with my eyes closed.

The next thing I remembered was waking up in the morning with Nate asleep across the bed on top of the covers with his clothes and shoes on. I slid out of bed and used the bathroom down the hall hoping not to wake him. I was in the kitchen unpacking dishes and looking for the coffee pot when Nate walked in the kitchen.

"I can't believe I slept all night with my clothes and shoes on."

"I know; I couldn't believe it either when I saw you this morning. I remember talking to you when you got in, but that's it."

Nate decided it would be easier to go get coffee and food, so he went to get food in the same clothes he slept in. Since he was getting food, I decided to go brush my teeth and shower before he got back. I was just stepping out of the shower when he got back. I quickly put-on leggings and a T-shirt and joined him in the kitchen. We had our coffee and breakfast at the kitchen table. After we finished breakfast, Nate finally took a shower. Nate was yelling my name from the bedroom.

I came running into the bedroom. "What's wrong?"

"What's wrong is we haven't christened our bedroom yet," said Nate with nothing on.

"And when we get through here, we're going to christen every room in this house," Nate declared, showing off what he was working with.

"Well, all right then, but don't start something you can't finish," I said as I walked into his arms.

"Oh, I can finish it," he laughed.

Chapter 15

I had just got into bed when the phone rang. I assumed it was Nate check-ing in, but the name on the phone display was who I had been expecting to call after I sent a wedding invitation to Gina and Melvin. I let the phone ring one more time and took a deep breath before I answered the phone.

"Hello."

The silence lasted so long one would have thought there was no one on the line, but I knew better.

"Eloise . . . I'm asking you to wait a few more years. When my boys get out of high school, I promise you I'll leave. Can you do that?"

"Wes, it's too late now. I got a chance to have all the things I've never had."

We were both waiting for the other to say something.

"If I left tonight, what would you do?"

"Don't do that…you know I would come, and you would grow to hate me if you couldn't be with your boys. Boy, you know you're not going to leave your family!" I laughed, and just like that the mood changed.

"You know you love me!" chuckled Wes.

"And you know you love me," I said. "Wes, do you believe in life after death?"

"What do you mean? I believe in God, Jesus, heaven and hell."

"Yeah, that's what I'm talking about. After we die, I believe we will live again either we will go to heaven or hell, and I'm trying to go to heaven, but you haven't made that easy," I chuckled. "We should have been together, sometimes I wonder if I would have had your baby, if Naomi had not gotten pregnant again; I wonder if we would have made it. Sometimes I wonder what my life would have looked like if we had not met. I like to think it was our destiny to be together, so maybe we will be together in the next life because my soul misses you."

"Maybe we will baby...maybe we will. I wasn't trying to hurt you, you know that, right?"

"Yeah, I know, but you did hurt me."

"So, are you trying to hurt me now?"

"No, I don't want to hurt you. I just do not want to hurt anymore. I want to know what it feels like to be number one for a change. I want to get married to a man who has never been married and I want to have babies with a man who has never had kids. I want to know what it feels like to be the first in somebody's life."

"I don't know what to say to that. I can't change the past, but I can love you in this life and the next one. Hey, I can be the first man to ask you to marry me in the next life. Eloise Ann Wallace, will you marry me in the next life?"

"Yes, Wesley Fisher, I will marry you in the next life," I laughed, while I wiped away a tear that fell from one eye.

Wes and I talked for a long time that night. We reminisced about the first night we were together and teased each other over who hit on whom first. Just before we hung up Wes told me that when he dreamed about us, he always dreamed about us when we first met and when we were together when his son died, and I told him that when I dreamed about us, I dreamed about our time together in the Altadena house. We talked about nothing and everything because we knew once we hung up that would be end of our love story. So, this was how it would end for us I thought. We were finally letting each other go at the same time.

Just before we hung up Wes told me to be happy and to remember that he would be waiting for me on the other side.

Chapter 16

"Happy Anniversary!" I said as I placed my leg across Nate's body. "Happy Anniversary, baby."

Nate turned on his side to face me, grabbed me in a bear hug and rolled on his back taking me with him. Nate groaned and rolled back to his side, dislodging me.

"Forget you!" I said rolling on my side away from him; before I could get out of the bed, Nate grabbed me holding me down in the bed.

"Where you going?" He asked.

"I'm getting my fat ass out of the bed."

"Yeah, that ass has grown in the last five years, but that's my ass," said Nate laughing and pulling on me until I leaned back lying my head on his stomach which was still flat.

"Nate lets' stay home today, not answer the phone and just chill. I don't want to do anything today; I just want to hang out with you."

"Sounds good to me, but don't you want to go out to dinner to celebrate?"

"Dinner is cool. Yeah, we can do that."

For the rest of the day, we lay in bed making love, watching TV and napping.

"You still want to go to dinner?" I asked Nate, not really wanting to get out of bed.

"Yeah, I want some Mexican food and a couple of Cadillac Margaritas," said Nate already sitting up to get out of the bed. Nate and I showered together, dressed and left the house to go to the restaurant.

During dinner, Nate had two margaritas; I had lemonade. Nate looked at me when I ordered lemonade instead of a cocktail.

"You not drinking tonight?"

"You know, just in case."

Nate took my hand and looked in my eyes.

"No, Nate I'm not, but just in case tonight is the night."

"It's going to happen, babe. Just relax, it will happen when it happens," said Nate.

"I know," I said looking back into his eyes.

We both tried to hide our disappointment that in five years of trying to have a baby we have not been able to have one yet. After the second year of trying to conceive, fear that it was not going to happen began to creep into my mind threating to take up residence. After each menstrual cycle we hid our disappointment and vowed to try again in a couple of weeks; and after trying to conceive I would hold my breath waiting to see if this time it would happen, and every month I did not get pregnant I pretended that it was okay. I would put a smile on my face like I was applying my makeup and would hold on to Nate when I told him that it did not happen this time, but maybe next time.

When I failed to get pregnant during out anniversary celebration, I was so disappointed. It was getting harder and harder to put on a mask for Nate, my parents and Ms. Mildred. The doctor assured me that I was physically able to conceive, so I figured that it must be Nate. We could not afford fertility treatments, so we just kept trying and trying.

Nate was on a long haul and would not be home for another few weeks, so if I was going to do what I had been thinking about doing, the clock was ticking. I was sitting in my family room drinking cinnamon whiskey in the dark with only the light of the TV illuminating the room. I had just finished looking at Naomi's Facebook page. I was sitting there looking at Wes's boys, then I was looking at Wes. Nate and Wes had similar features; it could work, I thought. I did not want this just for Nate; I wanted it for me also. I had always wanted a baby by Wes, but I did not have the courage to do it. Had Nate and I been able to have a baby of our own I liked to think that our baby would have been enough; but this way, I told myself I could have both a blood tie to Wes, and a child with my husband.

Older women told younger women, "A baby ain't gonna make a man stay." But that was not always true. Some men knew what it cost them and their children if they walked away, so they stayed; and because some men stayed, some women took a chance and got pregnant trying to manufacture a happily ever after. I needed a happy ending not only for myself but for Nate. We had both been unlucky in love and this was our last chance to be happy, and my last chance to have a piece of Wes that Ms. Nola nor Naomi could take from me. I told myself I was doing it for both Nate and I, but I knew I was doing it mostly for me. I remembered all those years ago thinking it was just sex when I decided to sleep with Wes, how wrong I had been. If I could not detach my emotions then, how would I be able to do so with his child? I had done everything I knew to do to forget about Wes. I had aborted a child, I moved out of my home, I married another man, but my thoughts somehow always looped back to him. Sometimes a smell, a song, or a glimpse of someone that looked like him would bring back a longing for those days when we were together.

Being without Wes was like having a part of me cut off, and the missing part ached, dull and persistent, almost dissipating until I bumped into a memory. Nate was the healing balm that I used to make life bearable; he allowed me to sustain my dignity, because without Nate it was just a matter of time before I went back to Wes and went back to living in the little space that I stole from Naomi and her kids. It was only 9:30 p.m. so I decided to see if Wes was willing to be with me. I dialed Wes's number hoping that he had not changed it.

"Eloise?"

"Hi, Wes. How are you?"

"I'm good. Are you okay?"

"I'm good . . . I was just sitting here thinking about you . . . us. Do you ever think about us?"

"What's going on with you, Eloise. Why are you calling me in the middle of the night?" asked Wes slightly perturbed.

"First off, it's not the middle of the night. It's only 9:30," I declared forgetting for the moment to be seductive. "I called because I've been thinking about you a lot lately. Do you ever think about me and the things we used to do?"?

Wes cleared his throat before answering, "Yeah, I think about you."

"Well, we can do better than just think, we could do something about it." I said breathlessly.

"Oh yeah, what can we do?" asked Wes, exhaling loudly.

"I can do that thing that you like me to do, remember?"

"Eloise, what the fuck are you doing. How am I supposed to go to sleep now?"

"Well at least you have Naomi. I don't have anyone here with me."

"I thought you had a husband?"

"We're going through some stuff right now. Can you help a sista out?"

Wes reluctantly complied and before we got off the phone, we had arranged to meet at a hotel the next day. Nate called me a few minutes after I hung up with Wes. I remembered him telling me that I sounded funny. We talked for about an hour and Nate said he was going to drive for another hour before he stopped to get some sleep. After I hung up with Nate, I was so wired that I could not sleep so I got out of bed and fixed another drink. What would Nate do if he found out? I did not want my husband to leave me, but I could not keep hoping against hope for a baby.

Most couples would try to convince themselves that it did not matter if they did not have a baby, but neither of us told that lie to ourselves or to each other. The disappointment each month was crushing, threatening to break us. Every month I had to pretend not to see the disappointment in his eyes while hiding my own disappointment from him.

That night I dreamt that Wes and I were together again in my house in Altadena. We were in the backyard getting ready for a party. Wes was mowing the lawn in the backyard, and I was rearranging the patio furniture. While we were in the backyard Mom, Dad, Ms. Nola, Gina and Melvin came into the backyard. I woke up just as Mom and I were going into the house to get the baby.

When I woke up the next day it was still dark. I did not have to take the early train today I would be taking a much later train, but I woke up early out of habit. I was sitting in the kitchen having a cup of coffee going over the scenario again. I had to play the disgruntled wife today and hope against hope that it was only going to take one time for Wes to impregnate me, because I did not know how I was going to feel after being physical with Wes; hopefully, I would walk away and not want to go back.

When it was time to meet Wes, I sat in the car thinking in another year or two I would be too old to try anymore, so time was running out for Nate and me to have a baby. I did not want to be an old parent like my parents were with me. Mom and Dad assumed they would never have a child; it was not until Mom was going through the change of life that I came along. Mom told me stories of how people thought she was my grandmother instead of my mother, and I did not want a baby that late in my life. I started the engine and pulled out of the driveway hoping this would work.

I checked into the hotel, and texted Wes the room number. I was waiting for him in a lace bra and panties set. When Wes knocked on the door, I opened the door hiding my body behind it. He walked into the room cautiously, when I closed the door exposing my body, Wes yelped, "Damn, girl!"

I whirled around giving him an eye full. Wes immediately took off his jacket and sat down on the bed.

"So, what's going on with you, Eloise?"

"You wanna talk now, really?"

"You that hot, you can't tell me what's going on?"

"Yes, I'm that hot," I said as I stood in front of him and unhooked my bra and slid my panties off.

After all this time, the hurt, pain and disappointment that I had gone through with Wes, making love to him was still good. I closed my eyes and tried to think about Nate and the family we would have if this worked, but thoughts of Nate and our family quickly fell away. Soon I felt myself holding on to Wes, not wanting to reach a climax just yet, not wanting it to end. Once I opened my eyes and Wes was looking at me like he was trying to figure out a puzzle. I held his gaze for as long as I could; I closed my eyes trying to shut out that desperate feeling that once again, I was going to lose myself to this man.

Wes and I did not talk again until after both of us were satisfied.

"So, why now?" asked Wes as he propped himself up on his elbows so he could get a better look at me.

"I don't know, Wes. I just wanted to be with you. Nate and I are going through something right now, and I thought I could have my cake and eat it too, just this one time."

"So, I'm being used?" he laughed. "Okay, use me up." Wes laid back with his arms spread wide opened. Wes laughed loudly and I began to laugh with him.

That afternoon and night Wes used me, and I used him.

That night with Wes was like so many other nights we shared, a warm dark embrace, where I could lean all the way back without being afraid of falling. As soon as the dawn's light drifted into the room that dull ache of missing Wes began. This time it was me looking at him like he was a puzzle that I could not figure out. I was in the shower when he came into the bathroom and stepped into the shower without a word. Water mingled with tears as I looked, into Wes's face, in that moment I wished that Wes and I could have left that room and the separate lives we had built for ourselves and just be us. I knew that we could not be happy with so many broken lives left in our wake. I pulled myself together and prepared to leave again the man who would always have my heart.

Wes drove me to Union Station and insisted on walking me to the train depot, when he spotted a coffee shop; he bought coffee and croissants. We were seated in big art deco club chairs, drinking coffee and munching on our croissants when Wes asked if we were going to see each other again.

"I wish we could, but I need to try and work it out with Nate," I said.

"If you don't work it out with your husband, call me. I don't mind being used." Wes got up threw his coffee cup in the trash and kept walking.

On the train ride, I had plenty of time to think. I thought I would feel guilty, but I did not. I did not want Nate to find out and I did not want to get a divorce. I really did love Nate, but if he left, I would not feel like a part of me was missing like it felt when Wes left. When I got to my stop, I breathed a sigh of relief, my car was still there. I had never left my car overnight, and I had not intended to last night, but I wanted to stay and so did Wes.

Nate was not due to be back home until after my period, so I would know if I was pregnant when he got home. Wes called the following week to see if I needed his services. I told him that I was confused, and I needed time to figure out what Nate and I were going to do.

I woke up the morning that I should have started my period, ran to the bathroom, peed and checked the toilet tissue after I wiped---no blood, not even a hint of blood. I could barely keep from smiling as I brushed my teeth, showered, dressed and almost skipped to my car. On the train ride to work I kept telling myself it worked. Nate would be home next week, so if I had not had a period by then I would take an early pregnancy test.

The day before Nate came home, I had taken an early pregnancy test, and it was positive. I was sitting on the tub in the bathroom thinking now we could live our lives. Nate and I would be a family, and I would have a piece of Wes to hold and love every day. I sat there praying that God would not let what I did harm my baby.

Nate was home by the time I got home from work.

"Hey, honey, I'm home!" I yelled as I walked through the door making a beeline to the kitchen. Nate was lying on the couch in the family room.

"Hey, baby," said Nate as he got up from the couch to kiss me. "I made dinner. Are you hungry?"

"Yeah, thanks. It smells good."

"The chicken is in the microwave and the mashed potatoes and vegetables are in the pots on the stove."

I used the bathroom and changed into my pajamas before making my plate.

"It's good. Thanks, baby."

Nate was back on the couch, watching TV. I was sitting at the kitchen table smiling to myself. I wanted to give it one more week before I told Nate that I was pregnant.

Nate was only home for three days before he was back on the road. For the next few weeks, I held my breath, afraid I would wake up having started my period. I made a doctor's appointment and was elated when the doctor confirmed that I was pregnant. Nate would be home in two days, and I was excited to tell him that he was going to be a dad.

The Saturday that Nate was due to be back home, I had Mom and Dad come down for the weekend and I went to pick up Ms. Mildred too. Ms. Mildred and I were sitting at the kitchen table having lunch when Mom and Dad arrived.

"Hey Mom, Dad, how was the drive?"

"It was fine, baby girl," said my Dad as he speed walked to the bathroom. Mom gave me a quick peck on the cheek and asked if she could use the master bathroom.

Mom and Dad were surprised to see Ms. Mildred when they came into the kitchen.

"What's going on?" asked Mom after hugging Ms. Mildred and looking at me. "Sorry, Mildred. How are you?"

"I'm fine, but I'm wondering the same thing now that I see you two," said Ms. Mildred.

"How're you doing, Mildred?" asked Dad as he patted Ms. Mildred's shoulder and sat down at the table. Mom took a seat at the table and folded her arms across her chest.

"Mom, Dad, are you guys hungry? Do you want something to eat or drink?" I asked.

"I'll get something to drink in a minute but first what room are we in?" asked Dad.

"You guys are in your usual room. Do you want me to get your bags out of the car?"

"Naw, I'll get them in a minute," Dad got up and went to the family room and turned on the TV. Mom, Ms. Mildred and I remained at the kitchen table. Mom was making herself a sandwich, and I was pouring her another glass of iced tea when I heard the front door being unlocked.

"Hey . . . hi everybody. What's going on?" asked Nate when he entered the kitchen.

I walked over to Nate and gave him a kiss. Nate hugged and kissed my Mom because she was standing by the island closest to him, then he went to the kitchen table leaned over and kissed his grandmother, then went to the family room to shake my Dad's hand. Nate came back into the kitchen and asked again what was going on for the second time.

"Nothing going on. Do you want something to eat?" I asked.

"Naw, I'll get something to eat after I take a shower. I'll be back in a minute."

Dad was on the couch dozing with the TV on, Mom, Ms. Mildred and I were in the backyard lounging when Nate came out and sat next to me.

"OK, what's going on?"

"Give me one minute." I got up and went into to the house to wake up Dad and brought him outside. Dad sat at the patio table because there was not enough room on the lounge.

"Dad, bring your chair over so you can hear."

When Dad scooted over to the group I stood up and pulled Nate up with me and placed his hand on my stomach. Nate looked at me, and I just smiled and shook my head up and down. Mom started screaming and jumped up clapping her hands. Ms. Mildred struggled to her feet, and Dad got up. Nate hugged me and turned around and hugged his grandmother. We all took turns hugging each other before we took our seats again. Then I was bombarded with questions after questions. How many months, when did I know, when is the baby due, how do you feel, have you been to the doctor?

After all the questions had been answered, Nate and Dad decided to put some meat on the grill, Ms. Mildred remained in the yard with my Dad and Nate while Mom and I went inside to see what we could make to go with the steaks.

Sunday morning Mom and Dad got on the road early to beat traffic; Ms. Mildred stayed until Monday. Sunday morning Ms. Mildred and I went to church; Nate stayed home to rest. After church Ms. Mildred and I stopped at my favorite store. When we got to the baby section, we looked at the clothes, but did not buy any baby clothes because superstition dictated that we wait until I was further along in my pregnancy. After we got home Ms. Mildred took a nap and I decided to put my feet up and watch TV in the family room. Nate came into the family room and sat next to me.

"I can't wait for the baby to get here," he said.

"I can't wait either. I hope I have a boy. What do you want?"

"I would love to have a son, but a girl would be cool, too. I almost gave up on the baby thing," confessed Nate.

I took Nate's face in my hands before I told him I almost gave up, too.

My pregnancy was brutal. I had morning sickness every day for almost three months, and somedays the morning sickness would last most of the day. Some days I would get to work and look down at myself and wonder what the hell was I thinking about when I put that dress or blouse on. Some days I looked like I was going fishing instead of going to work. One day I was in the elevator on the way up to the cafeteria. The elevator was packed as usual and Gina got on the elevator and looked at me and then my stomach. When we got off the elevator to go to the cafeteria, Gina and I hugged.

"I didn't know you were pregnant! How many months are you?" asked Gina as she let me go and stepped back to look at me.

"I'm seven months," I said smiling.

Gina and I talked as we went to the cafeteria, got our food and got back on the elevator to go back down to our courtrooms.

I knew that Wes would be calling after Gina saw me, so I was not surprised when he called a few weeks later. It was during my lunch hour at work when he called me on my cell phone.

"Is it mine?"

"Hello, Wes, how are you? I'm fine, thank you."

"Are you having my baby?"

"No, Wes. I'm having my husband's baby."

"If you're seven months, then that could be my baby."

"I was pregnant before we got together."

"I can count, can you?"

"Look, I got work to do, so let me put your mind at rest. I am a married woman having my husband's baby."

"You were a married woman when I fucked your brains out seven months ago!"

"OK, if this is your baby, what do you think Naomi would do?"

That must have caught him up short because there was a pregnant pause.

"So, I guess you were using me to get what your punk ass husband couldn't give you. When you have your baby, I want a DNA test and if you don't let me test my baby, then I'll have to ask your husband if I can test my baby."

"Wes, why are you tripping? You're not going to leave your family for me, or my baby so why are you tripping?"

"I'm tripping, because if it's my baby I want to know, because if that's my seed I have a right to know."

"You didn't give a fuck when I aborted your baby years ago, so why would you care if this baby is yours?"

"That's not true, Eloise, and it's damn sure not fair. That abortion was your choice."

"Fuck you, Wes," I said just before I hung up.

Wes's phone call did not upset me as much as I thought it would, because I knew Wes was as boxed in as I was; I knew he could not make good on his threat.

My Courtroom Assistant threw me a baby shower a week before my last day. Gina was there and brought me a ton of baby clothes. I could not help but think about how we got Melba's clothes washed and put up after the baby shower I threw for her. I was so grateful that my co-worker threw me a shower, but Gina should have been the one, Gina should have still been my best friend.

I missed my friend and I wished I could see Melba and Isaiah grow up; so, on the last week before maternity leave, I asked Gina if we could have lunch. Gina and I went to our favorite salad place and sat in the court-yard of the food court.

"Gina, I just wanted you to know that I miss you, and I wished we could have remained close."

"I do, too. I'm sorry that I stopped being your friend. I think about you all the time. I feel bad how this shit turned out. I'm so sorry, Eloise."

"I just hate that I don't get to see your kids grow up, and you won't get a chance to see my baby grow up."

Gina looked down at her plate and then looked up at me.

"I never would have thought that you would not be in my life or me in yours. I don't know what we can do."

"I don't throw people away, Gina; but that's what I did because I was hurt that you and Naomi were becoming friends. I just wanted you to know that I still consider you my friend, and I love you, Gina."

"Eloise, I love you, too!"

Gina retrieved her purse from the back of her chair, got her cell phone out and showed me pictures of the kids for the remainder of the lunch hour.

Nate decided to take off work the last month of my pregnancy. It was so nice being at home waiting for the baby to come. The baby's room was painted a pale pink with large black polka dots on one wall. A vin-tage dresser with a changing pad on top was on the same wall as a book-case stuffed with animals, books, diapers, wipes and cream. The crib was in front of the window but not too close, in case of drafts. The only other thing in the room was a wooden rocking chair.

The first week of my maternity leave consisted of me eating and sleeping. I did not realize how taxing the commute was and what a phys-ical toll it had been taking on my body. The second week we waited for

Ruby Pearl to arrive, Nate and I would take late afternoon walks; we would sit in the backyard and listen to music or watch television on the couch in the family room. One night we were watching TV, I got up to use the bathroom. I thought I had to pee, but I could not stop peeing. I called my Mom and told her what was going on, and she told me that it was my watering bag leaking; she asked if I was in pain, I told her that my lower back hurt a little bit. Mother told me to call the nurse's help line and see what they thought. After getting off the phone with the nurse, I went back in the family room and nudged Nate awake.

"Nate, wake up."

"I'm not asleep," said Nate yawning.

"We might be having a baby tonight."

"What? Okay, lets' go!" Nate jumped up from the couch, looking around for something.

"Hold on. I'm not ready yet." I told him what Mom and the help nurse said.

"So, what do we do now?"

"We can go to bed and try and get some sleep; the baby may not come until tomorrow. If my water breaks or the pain gets stronger and the timespan between contractions get shorter, we can go to the hospital."

Nate and I went to bed and slept for a few hours. I woke up soaked; my water broke while I was sleeping. Nate got dressed and pulled the sheets and cover off the bed while I cleaned myself up and put on a clean dress.

"How are you feeling?" asked Nate.

"My back hurts, but it's not too bad."

"Are you ready?" He asked.

"Yeah, ready or not, the baby's ready."

It was the wee hours of the morning, so no one was on the road, Nate got me safely to the hospital. We got checked in and waited 32 hours for little Ruby to come. Mom and Dad made it the next day just after 1:00 p.m. By 8:30 p.m., Mom and Dad went to our house to get some sleep. Nate slept in the chair in my room and I read a book I packed and slept off and on. The nurses came to check to see how much I had dilated, but I just could not dilate beyond three centimeters. The next morning Mom and Dad came back, and Mom became unglued. Mom demanded to see my doctor and to know why they would let me lay this long in labor.

After the doctor had made his rounds he came into the room and explained that the baby was fine and not showing any signs of distress, but he too was concerned that I had not dilated beyond three centimeters. The doctor came back an hour later and checked me and decided it was time for a C-section. Mom and I looked at each other giving each other the all-knowing look that it had really been Mom's idea, but I had to wait an hour for the doctor to convince himself that the C-section was his idea.

Ruby Peal Collins was finally delivered via C-section. She was 7lbs, 13 ounces, 21 inches long and with a head full of curly black hair. I was happy but exhausted while Nate, Mom and Dad were oohing and awing at the baby.

The night before I was to be released from the hospital, I convinced Nate to go home and get a good night's rest because I would need him to be fresh so I could get some rest tomorrow in my own bed.

The nurse had just brought the bottle for Ruby's feeding when Wes walked into the room with a big bouquet of flowers.

"Wes, what are you doing here?"

"I came to see my daughter."

"How did you know that I had my baby?"

Wes completely ignored my question and went around the bed so he could get a better look at Ruby. I watched Wes look at his daughter and all the tension between us melted. Wes asked if he could feed her and I handed his daughter to him. He sat down and gave her the bottle. He was smiling as she finished her bottle and he burped her. Wes kissed his sleeping daughter and placed her in her bed.

"Eloise, whether you want to admit it or not, I know she's mine. I'm not here to cause you any trouble, but I would like to see her from time to time."

"I can do that."

"Why would you name my daughter Ruby Pearl?"

"Because she's more precious to me than rubies or pearls."

"Yeah, she is."

Wes and I agreed that I would send him pictures and we would meet when she got old enough so he could see her in person. Wes told me that he loved both me and Ruby, kissed both of us on the forehead and left.

Chapter 17

My Mom used to tell me not to lie or steal, because there was nothing worse than for people to think of you as a liar or a thief, because of that I grew up hating liars and thieves. Funny how I did not hate myself, because that is exactly what I had become a liar and a thief. I have been lying to everyone I cared about: Nate, Ms. Mildred, Mom, Dad and Ruby, and I stole Wes's daughter from him.

Ruby was five years old, and she loved her dad, and Nate loved her with a passion that only a father could have. After Ruby was born, I did not go back to work for almost a year. Valeria and Charlie had moved to Victorville, and Charlie was now a truck driver. Charlie had followed through with Nate's suggestion and had contacted the trucking company that Nate worked for. Nate's company hired Charlie and paid for his training. Nate and Charlie became very close because Nate had not written Charlie off like so many others had, instead he encouraged Charlie and took him out driving in the desert so he could pass his driving test. Just before I was to go back to work Ms. Mildred moved in with us under the guise that we needed her to babysit Ruby, but the arrangement was more for Nate's peace of mind than for securing a babysitter. Valeria had already agreed to babysit Rudy. Valeria and I had decided that Ms. Mildred would watch Ruby alone until about 8 a.m., then Valeria would come over and help until about an hour before I got home, but more often, than not Valeria would still be at the house when I got home, especially if Ruby was still awake, or Charlie was on the road.

The first few years of Ruby's life was easy for me to keep my promise to Wes. Sometimes I would meet Wes at a park down the hill in Fontana or Rancho, and sometimes he would meet me at a park in Hesperia. When she was younger, he would hold her and play with her until we had to leave, but because Ruby was older now Wes would just sit and watch her play on the swings or go down the slides. Sometimes if she were asleep when I arrived, he would run his hand lightly over her face like a blind person trying to get an impression of who she was. Those visits were becoming harder and harder to arrange and to get through. Wes was living through what I had had to live through in the beginning of our relationship. He was on the outside looking in, watching someone he loved live, their life without him. It was hard for me to watch him suffer because I knew how it felt.

I was as happy as I could be, having made the decisions that I had made in my life. Ruby was a happy, well-adjusted little girl who brought so much joy to my life; she gave me the strength to live my life. Prior to Ruby, going to work, eating, sleeping and waking up to do it all over again was becoming increasingly impossible; but after Ruby, even the most ordinary day was a day filled with wonder and joy because I got to see the world through the eyes of my daughter. Sometimes I could see the wheels in her head spinning as she tried to figure out how something worked. Ruby made everything new and exciting. It was on one such date that Ruby and I were in the backyard picking tomatoes, weeding and watering the garden. Ruby was picking cherry tomatoes and putting them in her mouth.

"Ruby, let me wash them first before you eat them, OK?"

Ruby laughed and said okay with her mouth stuffed with tomatoes as the juice ran down her chin. I washed a total harvest of six cherry tomatoes with the water hose and put them in Ruby's blouse that she lifted up by the ends to use as a pouch to hold them. Ruby ran from the side yard to the backyard where Ms. Mildred was sitting.

"Granny Grand, I got tomatoes for you!" Ruby sang.

I had finished watering the vegetable garden and was watering my roses and other flowers in the garden when Ruby ran back to me.

"Mommy, Granny Grand won't wake up."

"She's tired, baby, let her sleep," I said as calmly and matter of fact as I could. I knew Ms. Mildred would not be waking up on this earth again. Ms. Mildred was in her late-eighties and had congestive heart failure. Nate and I knew this day would come sooner or later. I gave Ruby the garden hose and told her to water the roses until I turned the water off. When I rounded the corner, I saw Ms. Mildred sitting in her rocking chair with her head slumped over, cherry tomatoes were scattered around her feet. I felt for her pulse but could not find one, I put my hand under her nose knowing that I would not feel her breath. I turned off the water hose before calling out to Ruby.

"Ruby, let's go inside, now." I shouted.

"Aww, Mom do I have to?"

"Yes, we're done, let's go inside. You can watch TV or play in your room."

Ruby stomped inside and went to her room. I went inside and got my phone off the kitchen counter. I went back outside and pulled up a rocker next to Ms. Mildred. I called Valerie and told her Ms. Mildred had passed away in the backyard, and I needed her to pick up Ruby so I could call the paramedics. I sat there with Ms. Mildred and took her hand in mine. As I sat there waiting for Valerie to come, I thanked Ms. Mildred for loving me and Ruby. I told her how hard this was going to be for Nate, but Ruby and I would try to ease his pain. I told her what a good man she raised and told her because of her I had a good man and Rudy had a good father.

"I'm gonna miss you, Ms. Mildred, and I will never forget you," I sobbed.

Valerie and Charlie came in the backyard having come through the side gate. Valerie was already crying; she put her arms around Ms. Mildred's shoulders, causing her to launch forward. Valerie and I pushed her back securely onto the rocker. Charlie asked where Ruby was. I told him Ruby was in her room playing, and Nate was still on the road. Charlie wanted to know when he was coming home.

"I think he's due home in three or four days, I'm not sure, but I don't want to tell him while he's on the road. If you guys can take Ruby to your house, I'll call the paramedics."

Valerie started wiping her eyes, trying to get herself together.

"Hi, Auntie Valerie, hi, Uncle Charlie," said Ruby standing at the sliding glass door.

Valerie turned her back to Ruby, crying even harder. Charlie went to Ruby and picked her up and closed the sliding glass door. I hugged Valerie and told her to come in when she could. I went into the house; Charlie and Rudy were watching cartoons in the family room and I went to Ruby's room to pack a few toys, crayons, coloring book and paper for her to take over to Valerie and Charlie's house. When I came back into the family room Valerie had made it into the house and was sitting on the couch with Charlie and Ruby.

"Ruby, how would you like to go get some ice cream?" asked Valerie.

"Yay! Can I, Mom, please?" squealed Rudy.

"Yes, you can." I answered.

Ruby jumped up off the couch, opened the sliding door and shot out the door before either of us moved. All of us jumped up and went to the backyard where Ruby was, she was touching Ms. Mildred's eyes trying to open them.

I grabbed Ruby and picked her up, and Charlie held on to Ms. Mildred's shoulders.

Ruby was looking at me asking me why Granny Grand would not open her eyes.

"She's tired, baby."

"But I want Granny Grand to come and get ice cream too," whined Ruby.

"Not this time, baby."

"But I want her to come, Mommy," Ruby said as she was squirming trying to get down.

"We'll bring her some ice cream back," said Valerie.

We held our breath waiting for a five-year-old to determine whether this was going to be an easy transition and if we were going to have to take her out of the house kicking and screaming. Ruby looked at each one of us and said okay and that we could get Granny Grand two big scoops of vanilla ice cream because vanilla is her favorite. I gave Ruby a kiss which was a mistake because Ruby wanted to give Granny Grand a kiss goodbye, too. I put Ruby down and she tiptoed over to Granny Grand not wanting to wake her up. Ruby kissed her on the cheek.

Charlie and Valeria walked Ruby out the side yard. I heard Ruby telling Charlie and Valeria that strawberry was her favorite, but she liked vanilla, too. After they left, I called 911 and sat next to Ms. Mildred until the paramedics arrived.

Nate made it home three days later. Ruby and I were on the couch in the family room when he made it home.

"DADDY!!!!" screamed Ruby and ran toward the front door. Nate walked into the family room carrying Ruby. Nate sat down next to me and gave me a kiss.

Nate sat on the couch telling me about his trip and as usual ending the story with, "I'm getting too old for this shit."

"Ooh, Daddy said a bad word," giggled Ruby.

"Yes, I did, but I shouldn't have." said Nate as he tickled Ruby.

Nate and Ruby were lying on the couch watching TV. After a while they were both asleep on the couch. I let Nate sleep, knowing that would be the last peaceful sleep he would have in a long time. I woke Ruby up and had her help me make dinner. I put all the seasoning I needed on the kitchen island and as I seasoned the chicken Ruby would hand me the seasoning like a surgical assistant. After we placed the chicken in the oven, Ruby washed her hands and went back into the family room with her dolls and played with them in front of the couch close to her Dad. I sat at the kitchen table hating to have to tell Nate that his grandmother was dead. The smell of the baking chicken woke Nate from his slumber.

Nate stumbled toward our bedroom. I heard him knock on Ms. Mildred's door.

"Hey where's my grandma?" asked Nate peeking around the hallway.

"Ruby, stay in the family room. Momma needs to talk to Daddy in our room for a minute, OK?"

"Ok, Mommy."

I took Nate by his hand and walked him into our bedroom.

"What's going on. Eloise?"

Once we got into our room, I closed the door and hugged Nate as I told him how his grandmother left this world. Nate made a sound that came deep from his soul, a sound you could imagine our ancestors made when they lost someone they loved to death or the auction block. Nate sat on the bed and put his head in his hands as he rocked back and forth and moaned.

A week and half later, Ms. Mildred was laid to rest. We took Ruby to the funeral after discussing whether we should or not. In the end we decided that she needed to say goodbye too. She sat in her father's lap and cried herself to sleep during the service. We had a small repast at the house. Mom and Dad drove down from Vegas. Valerie, Charlie and a few people from work came. No one came from Nate's side of the family. He and Ms. Mildred had lost track of the few remaining relatives they had left. Two weeks after Nate buried his grandmother he went back to work.

Our lives went back to their normal routine except Ms. Mildred was not there to greet us at the end of the day. Ms. Mildred was not there to remind us to water the garden; she was not there to have tea parties with, or to spend a warm summer night looking up at the stars. The house was quiet, wrapping itself in the sadness and stillness that death brings. I was placing Ms. Mildred's hand-crocheted tablecloth on the dining room table. I tossed the tablecloth up in the air watching it ripple and float gently down until it hit the table with its full force like a slap on my face. In that instant I knew Ms. Mildred would not want us to linger too long in our sorrow; I remembered her saying, "Trouble don't last always."

I sat at the table for a minute and reflected on Ms. Mildred's strength, how she lost her only daughter to drugs and raised her grandson while grieving the loss of her child; how she lived long enough to see almost everyone she knew and loved die; how she was a tower of strength but was soft enough to love and hold. Ms. Mildred lived a hard life, but she did not let life make her bitter. I thought about the first time I met her at the apartment wine and whine Friday night get-togethers; she was so warm and welcoming. Ms. Mildred loved life and she loved us. I could hear Ms. Mildred telling me to get up and take care of her grandson and her great-granddaughter, and while I was at it to take care of myself. Ms. Mildred would tell me black women do not have the luxury to wallow in their pain, or to give up. I could hear her tell me, "Baby, it's time to get up and get on with living." I knew that if I did not get up and get on with living, then my family would be fatally wounded, our home would be a place where pain greeted you instead of a place of peace and joy, so I decided to try on those really, big shoes Ms. Mildred left behind.

Chapter 18

"Daddy, I got one, Daddy, Daddy!" yelled Ruby.

"Okay, calm down. Let me help. Pull a little, reel in, relax. Hey, good job!" exclaimed Nate.

Ruby and Nate walked over to where Valerie and I were seated to show us the fish Ruby caught. Ruby and Nate were all smiles. After Nate and Ruby told the story of how the fish was caught, they went back to fishing.

"You don't fish?" asked Valerie.

"Naw, girl. I just come to get outside and relax while they fish. I hear Charlie is getting into fishing, do you go with him?"

"Yeah, I go with him. I like it, but I have never caught anything."

"Sometimes I go into the village and stop at a couple of antique stores, collectible shops, and there's a nice café that serves great food; I swear its gourmet. That's where we're going to have lunch if those two ever quit."

Valerie and I sat and talked and eventually dozed off. Nate and Ruby had packed up their gear and the catch of the day when they woke us up. Lunch at the Grizzly Café was excellent as usual. Nate slept in the truck while Valerie, Ruby and I checked out a couple of the cute little shops. After shopping I told Nate that I would drive home so he could rest. As I was driving home, I was listening to Ruby and Valerie talk about how cute the town was and how good the food was. I was listening to the soft breathing and occasional snore that escaped from Nate's mouth, causing Ruby to burst out laughing. Suddenly, it occurred to me that I was happy. I called Mom on the way home and Ruby told her Paw Paw and Grandma how she caught a fish. Nate woke up just as I dropped Valerie off at her house.

"Did you have a good nap?" I asked at I pulled away from the curb.

"Yeah, with the food and the heat, I slept like a baby."

"I know. Ruby kept cracking up every time you snored."

Soon I was pulling up to the house. I opened the garage with the garage door clicker so Nate could put the fishing poles up. I carried Ruby into the house and put her in her bed, hoping she would not wake up anytime soon. Nate came into the house and went to the kitchen to gut and clean the fish.

"Do you want to fry this for dinner tonight?" asked Nate.

"Which one of us gets the fish, because that's not big enough for all of us," I laughed.

"Well, what do you want to do with it?"

"Freeze it. Hopefully, the next time you go fishing, you'll catch enough to feed us."

"Ruby is going to be a pretty good fisherman one day," said Nate.

"To hear her tell it, she already is. Come on, lets' get a little Mommy and Daddy time in before she wakes up."

"I heard that," said Nate, "Let me finish with this damn fish...hey don't get started without me."

"Sorry, I can't promise you that...you better hurry," I laughed as I walked away.

Ruby was at my parents for a couple of weeks that summer and Nate was on the road. Wes and I were having dinner down the hill in Rancho Cucamonga at Victoria Gardens.

"How's Ruby doing at your parents'?"

"She's good. The first couple of nights was iffy, but she's good now. She spent a couple of nights with Brenda and the kids and there are plenty of kids in Mom's neighborhood for her to play with. Mom babysits some of the kids, so they come and play with Ruby. I call her every night and we talk about her day. She's not ready to come home yet; she said she'll let me know," I said chuckling at the thought of her letting me know.

"That's good. Sounds like she's having a good time."

"She is. How are your boys?"

"They're good. Cassius is trying out for the football team, so he is going through hell week, and Dante has a skateboarding crew he hangs with. They are both in summer school but that will be over soon. We're going to try to get a family trip in before school starts back."

"That sounds nice. We need to do that. You know, me and Nate."

"Yeah, I knew who you meant," Wes said, looking at me.

"Where are you going?"

"Naomi wants to go to Detroit for a family reunion."

"Have the boys been there before?"

"Yeah, when they were little. Cassius was big enough to remember, but Dante was just a baby."

Wes and I had dinner and drinks and anyone looking at us would have thought we had been married for years. Wes and I met that night for him to give me Ruby's birthday gift which was a giant teddy bear and a ruby heart necklace.

"That's really pretty. I'll let her wear it to church and on special occasions."

"Here, I got you something, too," Wes handed me a jewelry box.

"Wes, I can't. You know it wouldn't be right."

"What about us has ever been right? Take it, I want you to have it." He, said.

I opened the box and inhaled as I looked at a beautiful diamond encrusted heart necklace. The necklace had one big heart with two smaller hearts inside the larger one; one of the hearts was studded with black diamonds and the other was studded with rubies.

"It's beautiful, Wes, thank you. But why is one heart black?"

"The big heart is our love encircling our kids; the red one is for Ruby and the black one is for the baby we didn't have."

Wes must have seen the pain that passed through my body on my face.

"Hey...I just wanted to acknowledge our other child. I didn't think ..."

"Wes," I said, looking up into his eyes. "I didn't know you even thought about that baby."

"I think about all my kids. I think about the baby we didn't have, and Wesley Jr. I think about how old they would have been. I think about if we're doing the right thing by not telling everybody the truth about Ruby."

"Wes… we can't let anyone know the truth," I whispered.

"Eloise, I'm not going to say anything, but I just wonder if it's the right thing," said Wes I put the necklace on because I did not have anything else to say. "Thank you, Wes, I love it."

After dinner, Wes walked me to my car. That evening was magical with the white lights strung around the village shops. We strolled to my car enjoying the warm summer night, and the illusion that we were a married couple out for a nice dinner. We looked into the shops and talked about the kids as if they were ours alone, Naomi and Nate forgotten inconveniences.

When we got to my car. Wes kissed me on the cheek. After Ruby, Wes and I had never cheapened our feelings for each other by giving into our lustful desires, but tonight with the fantasy surroundings and the gift of the necklaces, I moved in close and touched Wes's arm and kissed him. Wes responded and pushed me against the car. The world fell away, and passion threatened to fulfill itself under the night sky in a shopping center parking lot.

Suddenly I heard people talking and stopped.

"You want to get a room?" Wes asked.

"No, I'm sorry, I..."

Wes backed up to give me some space. He looked down smiling.

"I told you, it's something about you."

"No, it's something about us," I said smiling up at him.

I turned to get into the car, picking up the teddy bear I dropped when we kissed. Wes stroked my arm with his hand.

"Are you sure?" he asked.

"I'm sure."

I tossed the bear on the passenger seat and got in the car and started the engine. I expected Wes to walk away, but this time Wes just stood there with a faraway look on his face. I smiled and waved, but he did not respond so I rolled the window down.

"Penny for your thoughts," I said.

"What...oh, I was just thinking about life. Hey, be safe getting home. Don't forget to send me a picture of Ruby with her necklace on."

"Okay, goodnight, Wes."

"Goodnight, baby."

On the drive home going up the pass, watching the silhouette of the mountains and trees glide by, I thought about that chance meeting at the party and how it changed everything, not only for me but for everyone I loved. Any other night, it would have been someone else, and I would have been living another life without Wes, Ruby, Nate. If I had not met Wes, would Gina be married to Melvin and would Melba have been born? If Wes had not broken my heart would I have met and married Nate? More importantly if I had not fallen in love with Wes, would I have had Ruby?

Who can say how life would have turned out? I never chose to love Wes but loving him was like breathing. I do not try to explain it or understand it anymore, because it is beyond any rational explanation. Loving Wes never made sense and it never would.

Just as I rounded the bend to do the last climb up the pass, the sight of a huge moon took my breath away, and all I could think of was how beautiful life was, regardless of how hard it got sometimes, and in that moment, I had an urge to tell Wes how grateful I was that I met him. I wanted him to know that I still loved him and always would, so I called him.

"Hey, is everything okay?" he asked.

"Yeah, I'm good. I just made it up the summit. I just wanted to tell you that I love you, and I wanted to thank you for loving me and thank you for giving me Ruby."

"Thank me? Thank you, baby for loving me."

"Do you ever wonder what your life would have been like if we had never met?"

"No, but sometimes I think about what my life would have been like if I had met you first."

"Wes…ever since we met, I've been trying not to love you…but I can't do it anymore. I'm still in love with you Wes."

"I love you too."

"I don't want to hurt Nate, he has been good to me and Ruby, but I'm not in love with him. I'm in love with you, and I'm tired of denying it. It's you, Wes, it has always been you. I tried to be happy, but Wes, I'm not happy. Remember when you found out I was going to marry Nate… you called and asked me to wait for you? Wes I'm asking you to leave now because I feel like we are running out of time."

"Cassius is sixteen, and Dante is eleven. We just have to wait six more years."

"You promise?"

"I promise you," said Wes.

Wes and I talked all the way home. We talked while I changed into my pajamas. I felt like our love was becoming a new thing. Wes was refreshing me with tiny droplets of hope, and that night we chronicled our lives. We laughed at the good times and became solemn remembering our past regrets, but we said goodnight hopeful that one day we would be together again.

Chapter 19

Ruby had been home for about two weeks, and Nate was just about to leave for a couple of weeks.

"How come I can't go?" asked Ruby

"I told you, Ruby, you're too little, so stop crying, or I won't bring you back nothing," pleaded Nate.

Nate picked Ruby up and walked to the front door, with me following behind them. Ruby gave her Dad a kiss and Nate kissed me, handing Ruby to me.

Ruby and I waved goodbye watching Nate pull off.

"Let's go to the park and then we can go eat at MacDonald's," I said, putting Ruby down.

"Yay!" said Ruby jumping up and down.

Ruby was playing with a couple of other kids at the park's playground. I was sitting on the bench smiling to myself as I watched the kids playing. After what felt like forever, Ruby ran up to me ready to go eat because the other kids had left. In the car on the way to MacDonald's Ruby fell asleep in her car seat, so I decided to go to the drive-through instead. Ruby and I ate a late lunch in the backyard and afterward watered the flowers and our vegetable garden.

Ruby and I went back into the house. I was on the couch reading my book, while Ruby was lying on the floor watching TV when my cell phone rang.

"Hello," I said somewhat surprised seeing that it was Gina calling.

"Eloise?"

"Yeah, Gina, it's me. What's up?"

"Eloise," said Gina, crying.

"What's wrong, Gina?" I asked sitting up.

"Wes has been shot!"

With those words, the world shifted, and I slid off the couch. After I retrieved the phone I dropped, I struggled to stand up. Wake up, I told myself, this cannot be happening. I walked over to Ruby and looked down at her sleeping face. I bent down to touch her because this could not be happening. I felt her soft round face, and she stirred, her eyes fluttered trying to open, but slumber won out as she rolled over on her stomach and turned her head away from me. I began to touch myself; this is real, this is real, I was saying to myself.

"Eloise, Eloise!"

"Yes, I'm here. Gina, is he dead?" I asked after I realized that my name was coming from the phone I had in my hands.

"No, he's not dead, but it's bad. Melvin and I are going to Detroit tonight. I just wanted you to know."

"Detroit?"

"Yeah, he was on vacation with his family. He was shot a couple of hours ago. Naomi just called to tell us about it. I got to go, but I'll let you know what's going on. I'll talk to you later, goodbye."

"Thanks, Gina. Goodbye."

I stood there with the phone in my hand. I remembered the world becoming very quiet. I could hear my heart beating in my ears. When my heart slowed down, I could hear Rudy's breathing, then I could only hear the ticking of a clock, then my world became completely quiet and still.

"God, please...please."

I stood there, begging God to spare Wes for a long time. It was Ruby hugging me that brought me back to myself.

"Momma, Momma, don't cry," said Ruby hugging me and crying herself.

I sat on the floor, and hugged her so tight, no longer crying, but weeping uncontrollably. I woke up to darkness, with Ruby lying next to me whimpering in her sleep.

"Wake up, sweetie," I said, shaking Ruby.

Ruby woke up and hugged me, telling me how I scared her.

"I'm sorry, I won't scare you like that again. Are you hungry?"

"Yes, can I help make dinner?"

"I don't feel like cooking, so lets' go get something to eat. What do you want to eat?"

"I want a hamburger happy meal, French fries and a strawberry shake!"

"Wow! Okay, let do it."

I got up turning on lights as I went to the bathroom to wash my face. Ruby was trailing behind me. I was washing my face when Ruby asked why my eyes were so puffy.

"I must have slept on my eyes," I said, not knowing what else to say.

After dinner, I let Ruby stay up and watch TV later than usual. It was almost 10:00 p.m. when I called my mother. After assuring my mother that everything was okay and apologizing for calling so late, I asked her if she could keep Ruby for a few days. I told my Mom that I would be there tomorrow around one.

"Mom, everything's fine. A friend of mine is sick, and I want to fly out and see her. Goodnight, and I'll see you tomorrow."

After I got off the phone, I picked Ruby up off the couch and put her in her bed. I made sure the doors and windows were locked, put the alarm on and went to my room. I called Nate and told him an old friend of mine was sick and may not make it, so I was going to leave Ruby with Mom and Dad for a few days and fly out to Detroit. Nate did not mention the fact that he had never heard me talk about this old friend; he just told me to be careful and let him know when I got to Mom and Dad's tomorrow.

After I got off the phone with Nate, I packed our bags. I slipped into Ruby's dark room careful not to wake her up or bump into anything. Ruby was hugging the teddy bear that Wes had given her for her birthday; she looked so peaceful, her world was still intact. As I was walking out the room with her clothes in my hands, Ruby stirred in her sleep and I stopped moving until she drifted back to sleep. With Wes so near to death I felt like the real me was floating around watching someone that looked like me pack and make plans while the real me had become untethered from my body. I wanted to fly away and find Wes or go back to the past and make different decisions, ones that would allow Wes to still be alive. After I packed, I could not sleep, so I mopped the kitchen and bathrooms floors. When there was nothing left to clean, I made myself a drink and retreated to my bedroom hoping the alcohol would lure me to sleep. I was propped up in bed sipping my second drink when I felt a gust of wind blow into the room. I knew before my mind could comprehend exactly what was going on. I didn't see him, but I felt his presence, and, in my head, I heard him say, "I'm okay, Eloise. Tell Melvin I'm okay." He was gone as quickly as he came.

"Now what? What do I do now? I'm done, Lord, I don't have it in me to go on." I sat in bed talking out loud to God. I wanted to scream and not stop. I wanted to surrender to the nothingness that I imagine insanity would bring with it; I wanted to simply fade to black.

I turned off the light on the nightstand and removed the pillows from behind me, lay flat in the bed looking into the void of my closed eyelids; in that void my body and mind floated as I contemplated giving up on life itself. I opened my eyes and propped myself up high enough to fumble around for my drink on the nightstand and sunk back down in my bed after finishing my drink. I can't...I can't keep going I thought to myself. I will never know if we would have been together was the last thing, I remembered thinking before drifting off into a drunken slumber.

The next morning, I woke up early, made myself a cup of coffee and sat in the backyard in the dark. I sat in the backyard long enough for the moon to fade as the sun in all its colors lit up the sky. I watched the birds flying around, so many different kinds of birds. Big black ravens or crows, mourning doves, hummingbirds and the little brown birds. The sun felt good on my face. I closed my eyes and felt the tears slide down my face. It was a perfectly ordinary day, a day in which I would have gone to work after I dropped off Ruby at Valeria's house because school was not open yet when I left for work. On the other side of my fence, I could hear cars driving up and down the street; life was moving along as if it did not matter that Wes was no longer one of the people enjoying this beautiful day. I decided that I would take Ruby to school so I could be alone with my thoughts. I called Valeria to let her know I was staying home today.

As I was making breakfast, my cellphone rang. I knew it was Gina before I looked at the screen. Not yet, I thought to myself, confirmation of Wes's death could wait until after I took Ruby to school. Gina called a second time before she gave up. I took Ruby to school, and I drove to a park I used to meet Wes in and sat in my car and called Gina.

"Hi, Gina. I saw that you called. I just could not answer because I was afraid of what you were going to tell me. How is Wes?"

"Eloise..." Gina said, as she was crying.

"I already know, Gina. It's okay. I know he didn't make it. Do you know what happened?"

"They shot him two times in his chest. He was just standing in the front yard of Naomi's mother's house. Naomi's brothers and cousins were in the yard, drinking and smoking, just hanging out when a car pulled up and started shooting. He died late last night. I didn't want to wake you, so I waited until this morning to call you."

"Thanks Gina, for letting me know. Please let me know when his funeral is. Gina, how is Melvin taking this?"

"Melvin is beside himself. I don't know how we're going to make it home."

"Tell him Wes came to me last night, and he told me he was okay, he told me to let Melvin know that he was okay."

I could hear Gina crying. When she was able to speak, she told me she would tell Melvin, and let me know what was happening when she knew.

I sat in my car, crying, feeling so lost, struggling to stay in the here and now, but wanting to go live in the darkest recesses of my mind, where Wes and I could live forever. A darkness overtook me; my eyes were open, but I was inside the darkest night where the pain of losing Wes filled me with despair, my mind was leaving me when I heard a voice say, "I will comfort the broken hearted. I will never leave you or forsake you." And as those words were being spoken, the darkness began to recede, and I was once again sitting in my car on a clear sunny day rubbing the necklace Wes had given me. Before I left the park to go home, I called my mother to let her know that I would not be coming because my friend had not lived.

"I'm so sorry, honey. How are you holding up?"

"I'm okay Mom. It was shocking to hear that someone that I once knew had died so unexpectedly. Thanks, Mom, for letting me drop Ruby off if I had to."

"You know me and Paw Paw love having Ruby with us. You let me know if you need me. I got to go and make your father's lunch. That man acts like he can't do nothing!" said Mom.

"You made him that way. Remember what you told me. Don't start nothing you can't keep up!" I chuckled, my heart feeling lighter for a brief, moment.

It was five weeks after Wes was killed before Naomi could put her husband to rest. It took almost three weeks for the autopsy to be done, then the body had to be embalmed in Detroit before it could be transported to California. Gina kept me in the loop of what was going on, and she told me the date of his viewing and funeral. I sent a big floral arrangement with no card hoping Naomi would not throw it out.

The wake was at Rose Hill Memorial Park in Whittier, California, which is a long drive from Victorville. I told Valeria that I would not be able to pick up Ruby until around 9:30 or 10:00 p.m. I had already said goodbye to Wes in my mind and heart, but I needed to see his body, so I would know that it was real, that Wes was lost to me forever. The hope that Wes and I would be together would not completely die; it flickered like a lit candle in a soft breeze, and I needed it to die, if life with Nate was going to be possible. I had left so little room for Nate in my heart when Wes was alive, and just before Wes was killed, I had almost pushed him completely out of my heart, because I was living for the day Wes, Ruby and I could be together, when we could be a family.

The day of Wes's wake was like any other day, except it was not. The frenzy of the morning getting Ruby ready for school, dropping her off was like all my other days, but that day I drove down the hill to visit my past. I decided to drive down early and look at my house in Altadena, then I would go to Gina's house and hang out with her until it was time to go to Rosehill where Wes's viewing would be held.

It took almost two hours to get to Altadena. I stopped at Jack in the Box and got an iced coffee and used the bathroom. It was still too early to go to Gina's house, so I stopped by a couple of thrift stores on Lake Avenue, within walking distance of Jack in the Box where I left my car parked. As I walked down the street to the first thrift store it was like walking back in time. A quiet peace came over me as I entered my first thrift store. I was reminded of the times I would be on the hunt for some treasure for our house.

I spent over an hour in the store. I bought a couple of funky earrings for me, and a miniature Windsor chair for Ruby's room. I was completely lost in the thrill of junking when I went to the next thrift store. I was enjoying myself. I was talking to the other customers in the store, laughing. Wes was not dead, and I was not married to Nate. I was thinking when I left here, I would go home and show Wes the treasures I found; that is what I was thinking as I browsed the store, and that is what I was feeling when I pulled into the driveway of the Altadena house. That is when reality collided with my fantasy that Wes was alive, and we were together.

I backed up out of the driveway and parked in front of my house. I had not told the tenant that I would be coming so I did not get out of the car. I wished I had, because I wanted to see the backyard, where Wes and I had so many parties. The front yard looked good; the grass was green, and the hedges were neatly trimmed. Wes would have been happy to see his yard looking so good, I thought, and that is when my heart skipped, and the hollow ache returned. Wes would never see his yard again and we would never be together again. I sat in front of the house wishing I could go back in time. If I had known the future, I would have stayed right here, playing house, foregoing my desire for a normal life. I would have lived my life with Wes in the murky shadows; anything was better than living on this earth without him. I should have fought harder for him; I should have matched Naomi baby for baby. Would that have made a difference? I should have ignored Naomi's second pregnancy like she ignored me all these years. She had to have known Wes was with me on those nights he did not come home. Maybe she played the game better because she grabbed the golden ring; she was his wife, and the mother of his children. All his possessions were hers; all I had were my memories. Ruby was legally my husband's child, but I knew the truth; she was our love child. She was proof that there was love between us and that I, too, had a place in Wes's heart. I was wiping fresh tears away when my cellphone rang. It was Gina, and I told her I would be at her place in a couple of minutes.

Gina and Melvin's place looked the same, except the front yard was littered with kids' bikes, a skateboard and a basketball.

Gina opened the door before I could knock. We hugged each other for a long time in the doorway. Finally, we released each other and walked into the house. I looked around, smiling, remembering all the times I had been in this room with my friend in happier days.

"I like it. You opened the living room to the kitchen, right?"

"Yeah, and we added on a small family room off the kitchen," said Gina smiling with tears glistening in her eyes.

Gina ushered me into the family room stopping to show me her kitchen.

After I told her how much I loved the renovations and her new family room, Gina and I sat on the couch in the family room.

"How is Ms. Nola doing?" I asked.

"Ms. Nola doesn't know; she has dementia and Naomi didn't have the heart to tell her."

"Wow, how long has she had dementia?"

"It's been a few years. Wes finally had to put her in a home, because she started wandering off from her house," said Gina.

We sat in Gina's family room for almost an hour. Gina told be how Melvin, Naomi and her boys were taking Wes's death. We decided to go get something to eat in Old Town Pasadena. We went to the same restaurant we all went to in the past. After we finished our meal we lingered at the restaurant, watching people walk past the plate glass window. Boy, how I missed Altadena, and the life I had there.

"You know Wes told Melvin that Ruby is...was his child," said Gina out of the blue, as we were sitting in what I thought was a comfortable silence.

"What?"

"Yeah, Wes was so excited that you were having his baby, and a girl at that."

"No, I didn't know, but I shouldn't be surprised. He and Melvin were like brothers," I said looking at Gina. "Did Naomi know?"

"No, I don't think so. If she did, we never spoke about it."

"Was Wes happy? I know he loved his boys, but was he happy with Naomi?"

Gina looked down, and then out the window before she answered.

"I think he and Naomi were happy."

"Do you think he loved me?" I asked, as a tear slid down my cheek.

"Yes, Eloise. Wes loved you and Ruby, but he also loved Naomi and his boys." Gina reached for my hands and held it, as we continued to watch the day slip away.

"I don't want to cause any trouble; I just want to say goodbye. I need to see him, just so it can be real. Can you tell Naomi that for me? I just want to see him today; I'm not going to the funeral tomorrow."

"Yeah, I can do that."

Gina insisted on paying for lunch, after which we got up to leave. When we got outside the restaurant the world took on a surreal quality. A golden glow enveloped the late afternoon sky.

When we got to Rose Hill, I parked in the main office parking lot and got directions from the receptionist as to where Wes's viewing was being held. Gina and I found the viewing room and I waited outside while Gina went inside to ask Naomi if I could come in. Gina was inside for so long I thought I was going to have to make a scene, because I was going to say goodbye to Wes with or without Naomi's permission. Gina and Melvin came out together. Melvin gave me a hug, but never released me; he loosened his hold on me enough for me to face Gina. Gina looked at me with furled brows and explained that Naomi did not want to be in the room with me, so she and the boys would leave the viewing ten minutes before it ended. She also did not want me hanging out in front of the door in case the boys came out and wanted to know who I was. I told Melvin and Gina I could respect that and to tell Naomi thank you. I told them I would be in the lobby downstairs and would wait until Naomi and the boys left. I took the elevator down to the lobby and waited for two hours before I could say my final farewells to Wes. While I was waiting, I called Valerie to check on Ruby.

"Hi, Mommy."

"Hi, Ruby, are you being good?"

"Yes, Mommy. We're going to have pizza and ice cream!"

"Okay, but eat your pizza, before you eat your ice cream, and not too much ice cream, so your tummy won't hurt, OK, Ruby?"

"OK, Mommy. What you doing, Mommy?" asked Ruby.

"I'm having dinner with an old friend, and then I'll be there to pick you up. Did you do your homework?"

"Not yet, Mommy."

"Uh huh...let me talk to Valerie."

"Thanks, Valarie for watching Ruby this late, but make sure she does her homework before you let her watch TV.

I called Nate, but he could not talk because he was just about to pull into a weigh station. He said he would call me later. I sat in the lobby and watched people checking in with the receptionist. I watched the grief stricken; the ones left behind. People were going into the back offices to make final arrangements, or attending viewing, as it was too late for funeral services. Rose Hill had coffee, tea, water and cookies set out for the bereaved, so I made myself a cup of coffee and stepped outside. A soft blue sky—still light enough to read a book by—had replaced the earlier golden hue and I looked up at the sky and spotted one twinkling star and the faint impression of the moon. Looking up at the sky reminded me that death was not the end; there was a heaven beyond the heaven I could see. Wes was not lost; he was in heaven with God, his son and the child we never had. I would miss him, but I knew I would see him again when it was my time to fly away. I went back inside, waiting for my time to say goodbye.

I was looking at Naomi's Facebook page when Naomi and the boys walked across the lobby and out the door. Cassius was tall and looked just like Wes; Dante looked more like his mother, but you could see Wes in him as well. Naomi walked stoically past me, with her boys flanking her. Naomi had one arm around Cassius's waist and one arm around Dante's shoulders, holding him close to her. Dante's head hung down as he sobbed. I watched them walk out into the night before I got on the elevator.

From the back of the room, the beautiful blanket of red roses that covered the lower part of the casket pulled me closer to it. I had not noticed that Melvin and Gina were still seated in the front seat, because all I could see was Wes's profile. I looked down at Wes's face; it looked like he was sleeping. I traced his face with my fingers. His skin was hard, having lost its softness in death. How many times had I woke him up with a kiss, if only a kiss would wake him now!

"I'm going to miss you, baby. I'll see you on the other side."

Melvin, and Gina walked me to the car. I assured them that I was able to drive myself home. On the drive home I let the hope of Wes go for the last time. Wes was no longer my future or my happily ever after.

Chapter 20

Today was a strange day, all day I felt compelled to relive a love story that was almost 30 years old. Usually when I thought about Wes, they were brief remembrances of a love that happened a lifetime ago; but today he was all I could think about and it felt like it was only yesterday that we were together. Wes has been dead six years, although I can still remember the sound of his voice whispering in my ears, or how he smelled when he held me in his arms, those memories were faint impressions compared to what I experienced today. Today's images and feelings were strong and vibrant, forcing me to relive them. His death was an ending and beginning for me. Gone was the naïve little girl that I was when I met him and standing in her place was the woman that had to live with that choice. The woman that I am today knows that given the chance, I would make the same choice again that night, knowing how much it would hurt me and knowing that I would lose in the end.

I get up from the couch stiff from sitting there for hours, it is almost 3:00 a.m., I cannot believe I spent the whole night reliving the past and yet it was cathartic I knew that I would not have any trouble falling asleep now. I turn off the TV and the light in the family room. I make sure the front door is locked and look in on Ruby. She has gone to sleep with her desk light on, again. I go over to her desk and turn off the light. The giant teddy bear that her Dad gave her for her sixth birthday is lying on the floor instead of sleeping with her like it did when she first got it. I look at her face which holds the secret of who's child she is in plain view if anyone knew to look. I turn and go to my bedroom, after using the bathroom and changing into my gown I stumble into bed, only to get out of bed to set the alarm. I am almost asleep when I realize that this is the year that we were supposed to be together. Ruby would be 12 in a couple of weeks, Wes and I had dinner a couple of weeks before her birthday six years ago. Wes promised me that night, that we would be together in six years, this is the anniversary of that promise! Is that why he was all I could think about today? Maybe, I said to myself, or maybe I was reading too much into a coincidence. Just as I drift off to sleep, I see Wes standing under a streetlamp with a glow surrounding him. His stretched out arms inviting me to come to him, just as I am about to step into his arms, he fades away leaving me hugging myself.

I slept in late the next day, waking up feeling a little out of sorts.

"Good morning, Mom."

"Good morning, Ruby."

"Mom, can you take me and Shanice to the mall today?"

"Do you have any money to go to the mall?"

"Well, I was hoping you could give me my birthday money, so I could buy something I really want."

"What makes you think I was going to give you any birthday money?"

"Come on Mom, I'm almost a teenager now so I'm old enough to buy my own birthday present."

"You're turning 12!" I exclaim.

"Exactly, this is my last year as a tween. After this birthday I will officially be a teenager," says Ruby, as she texts.

"You make a convincing argument, but I still need to think about it. I didn't sleep well last night, so let me have my coffee in peace."

"OK, Mom. I'm texting Shanice now, so we'll be ready wherever you are."

And that was how my day started, catering to the whims of a tween. I spent the day in the mall with Ruby and Shanice going in and out of stores watching them try on clothes. Eating at the food court and watching them watch boys whispering to themselves and giggling.

Two weeks later Ruby celebrates her birthday with three of her girl-friends having their nails polished at the nail shop I get my nails done at, then I drop them off at the movie theater; after the movie I pick up the girls and a couple of pizzas for the sleepover.

Nate made it home the next day after the girls had been picked up by their parents, so it was just the three of us at home when he decided to barbecue. Ruby and I are lying on a blanket in the backyard, she is looking at something on the cellphone she got for her birthday. I look up at the clouds and try to engage Rudy in one of her favorite things to do as a little girl.

"Over there, that looks like a turtle. See, there's the head, the shell and even a little tail," I say, arm lifted with my finger pointing to the cloud.

"I don't see it, Mom," says Ruby barely glancing at the clouds.

"Come on, Ruby, you're not trying. You used to see the animals."

"Yeah, when I was little," Ruby says, as she gets up and walks in the house.

Nate flips the hamburger patties on the grill, closes the lid and lays down next to me and asks where is the turtle?

"It's gone now," I say, giving up on the game.

"You know our baby girl is growing up."

"I know, but I still need a few more years, where we are her every-thing," I tell Nate.

"Not going to happen, so you better get used to it," Nate turns to face me and kisses me on the forehead.

I look up at the clouds again, sighing loudly. Nate chuckles and rolls on top of me and rolls again until I am on top of him. He gives me a couple of quick pecks on the lips and I give him a long French kiss.

"OMG, that's gross!" yells Ruby as she stands in the half opened sliding glass door.

Nate and I crack up laughing, and Ruby retreats, back inside the house.

"If we're lucky, we got another year or two before she's kissing boys," says Nate before he gets up to tend to the meat on the grill. I roll back on the blanket, close my eyes, enjoying the warmth of the sun. My fingers are rubbing the heart necklace that Wes gave me. One day I might stop wearing it, or maybe I think to myself, I will take it to the grave with the rest of my secrets.

Wes's death has changed me and how I move in the world. I have gotten closer to God and I find comfort in the gospel of Jesus Christ. Although, there is an emptiness that resides in my heart—a place so empty it aches—time and God's grace has eased the pain. There are times I can breathe deeply and there are times when the shallowest breath hurts.

Sometimes, a smell, or a song on the radio causes the memories of Wes to pour down on me like a flood and grief threatens to overtake me. It is at those times that I hear Ms. Mildred telling me to get up and keep going. Life is for the living; the dead can take care of themselves. I remind myself that Wes himself told me that he was okay. So, I get up and I keep living for Ruby, Nate and for myself.

I gave Wes my love with a depth and capacity that I have never given anyone before or since, and there is no shame for me in that. The love I have for Nate is different, as it should be, because each giving of yourself is different. There is an emptiness in Nate that I will never fill that is a void that only Malissa can fill and that is okay because I know I have a place in his heart, and he has a place in mine.

The End